THE ONLY LIVING BOY

TO SAVE A SHATTERED WORLD

by David Gallaher and Steve Ellis

PAPERCUTZ™

New York

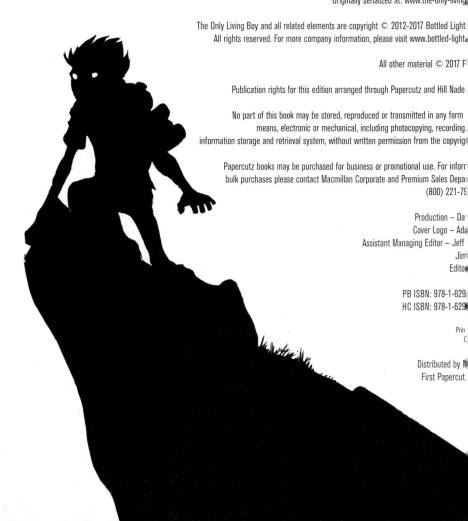

Dedicated to everyone out there
fighting the good fight.

THE ONLY LIVING BOY #5 "To Save a Shatter...

Chapte...
Writer/Co-Creator: Davi...
Artist/Co-Creator: S...
Color Flatting: Holley McKend, Jules Rivera, C...
Additional Flatting: David B. Cooper, Alliso...
Proofreading: Janel...
Lettering: Melan...
Assistant Editor: Emi...
Studio Assistant: Jen...
Production: Salina Ma...

Special Thanks to Grace Gordon and Sarah Sawye...

Originally serialized at: www.the-only-living...

Publication rights for this edition arranged through Papercutz and Hill Nade...

Papercutz books may be purchased for business or promotional use. For infor...
bulk purchases please contact Macmillan Corporate and Premium Sales Depa...
(800) 221-79...

Production – Da...
Cover Logo – Ad...
Assistant Managing Editor – Jeff...
Jim...
Edito...

PB ISBN: 978-1-629...
HC ISBN: 978-1-629...

Prin...
C...

Distributed by...
First Papercut...

CHAPTER NINE

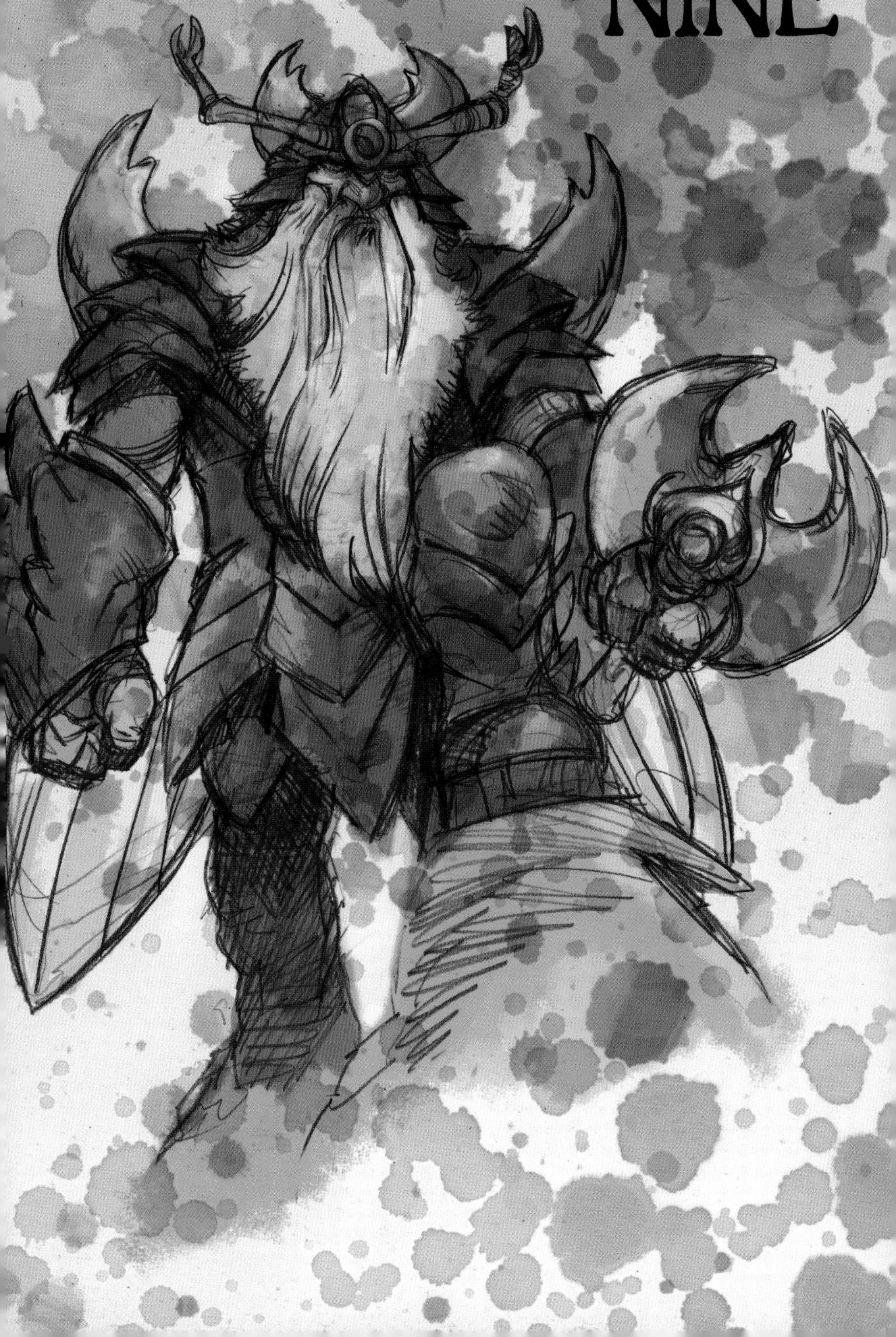

Previously in...

THE ONLY LIVING BOY

Staging a dangerous escape from the sinister lab of Doctor Once, Erik finds his freedom deep in the forest among the savage Alku. Appointed leader of this fierce tribe, Erik accidentally alerts Baalikar's nearby forces. With Kleef's guidance, Erik and his allies seek safety up North. In an effort to decipher Doctor Once's dying words, Erik travels alone through a forbidden swamp to find the answers he will need to defeat Baalikar. Stumbling upon an observatory, Erik discovers a colony of scientists that he is too late to save. Amidst the destruction, Erik vows to unite the forces of the patchwork planet together to stop Baalikar once and for all. Traveling to Mermidonia and the Groundling Empire, Erik convinces the tribes to join forces and save the Hive City of Sectuarius – but will he be too late?

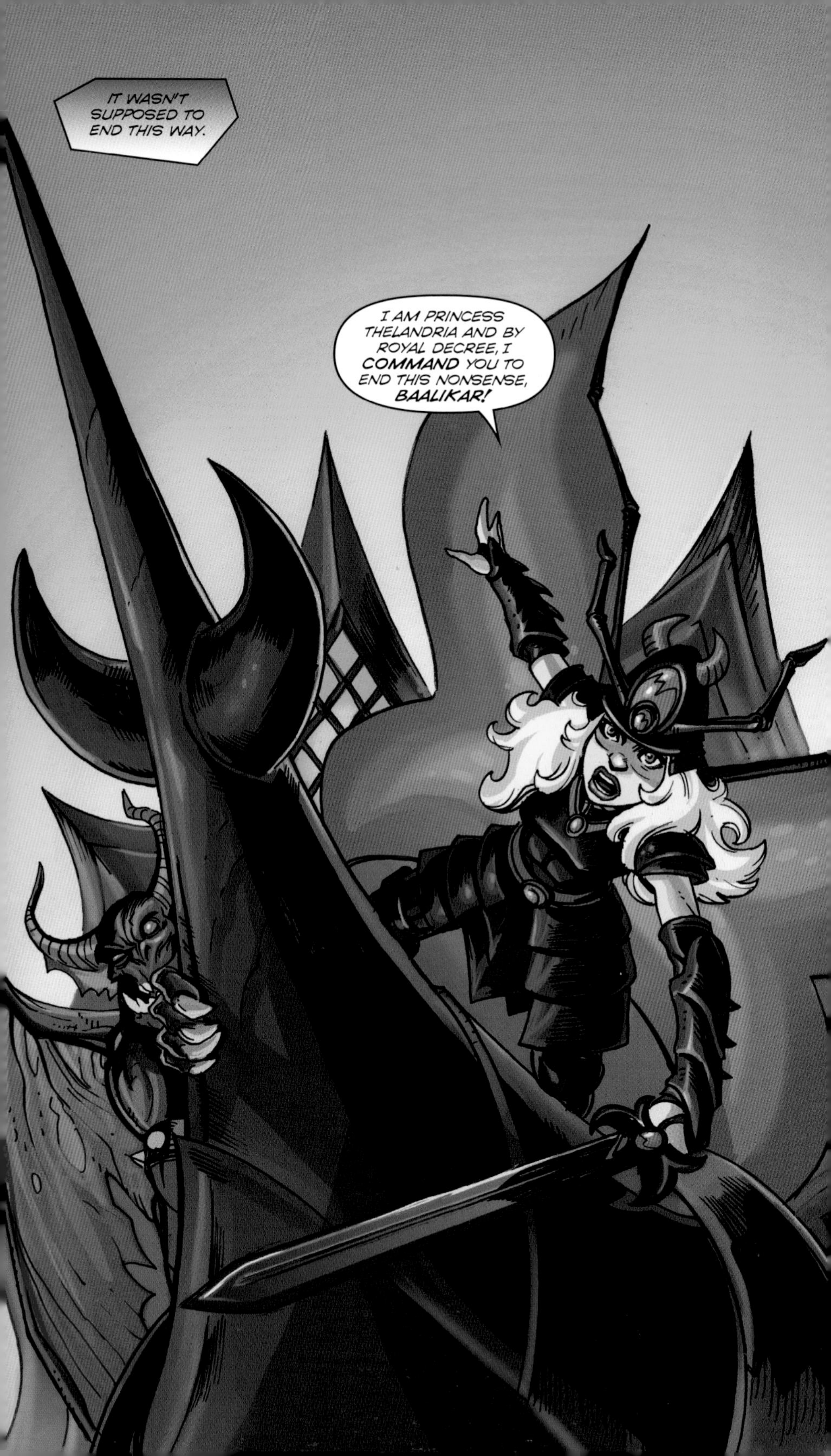
IT WASN'T SUPPOSED TO END THIS WAY.
I AM PRINCESS THELANDRIA AND BY ROYAL DECREE, I **COMMAND** YOU TO END THIS NONSENSE, **BAALIKAR!**

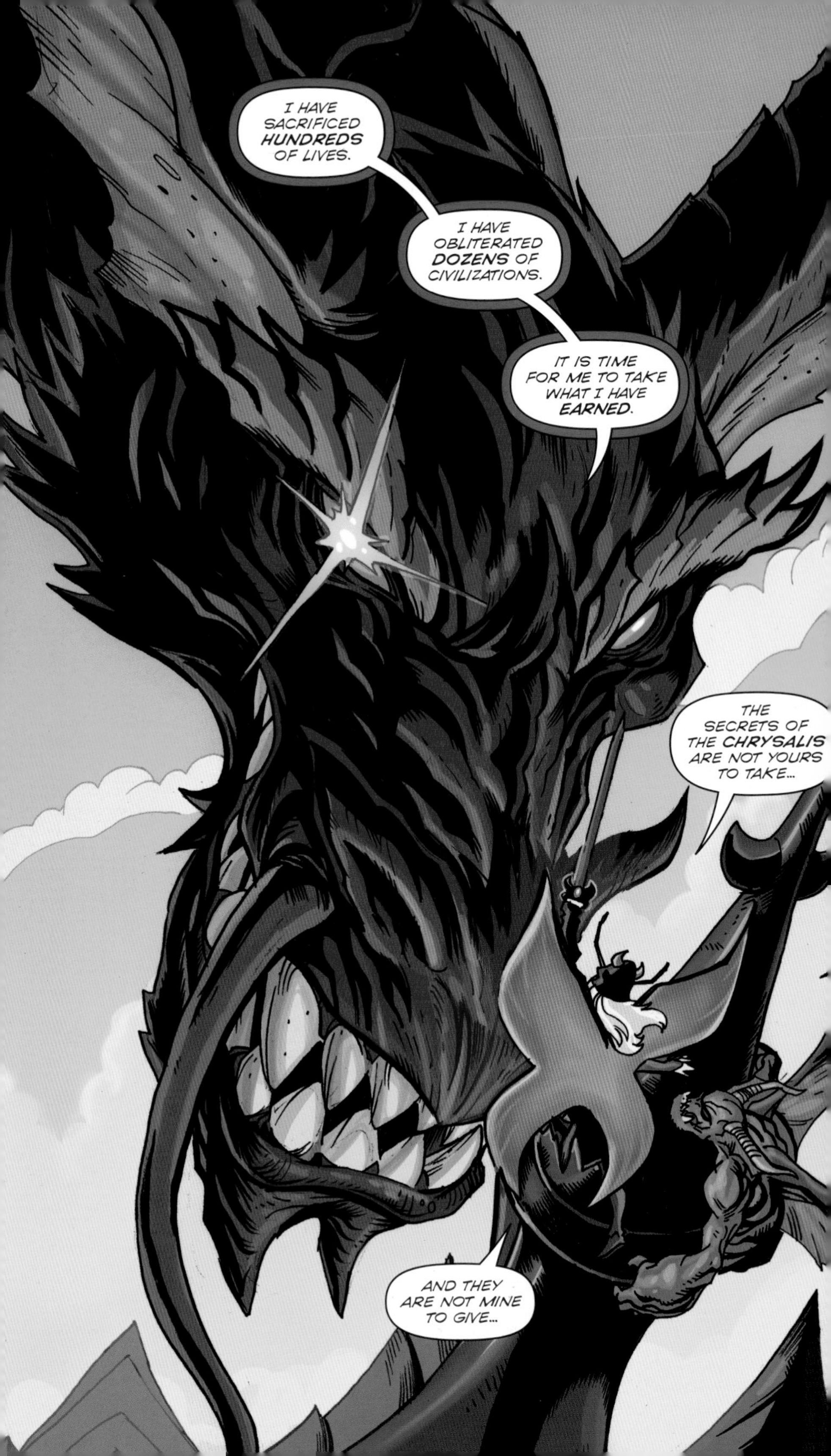
I HAVE SACRIFICED HUNDREDS OF LIVES.
I HAVE OBLITERATED DOZENS OF CIVILIZATIONS.
IT IS TIME FOR ME TO TAKE WHAT I HAVE EARNED.
THE SECRETS OF THE CHRYSALIS ARE NOT YOURS TO TAKE...
AND THEY ARE NOT MINE TO GIVE...

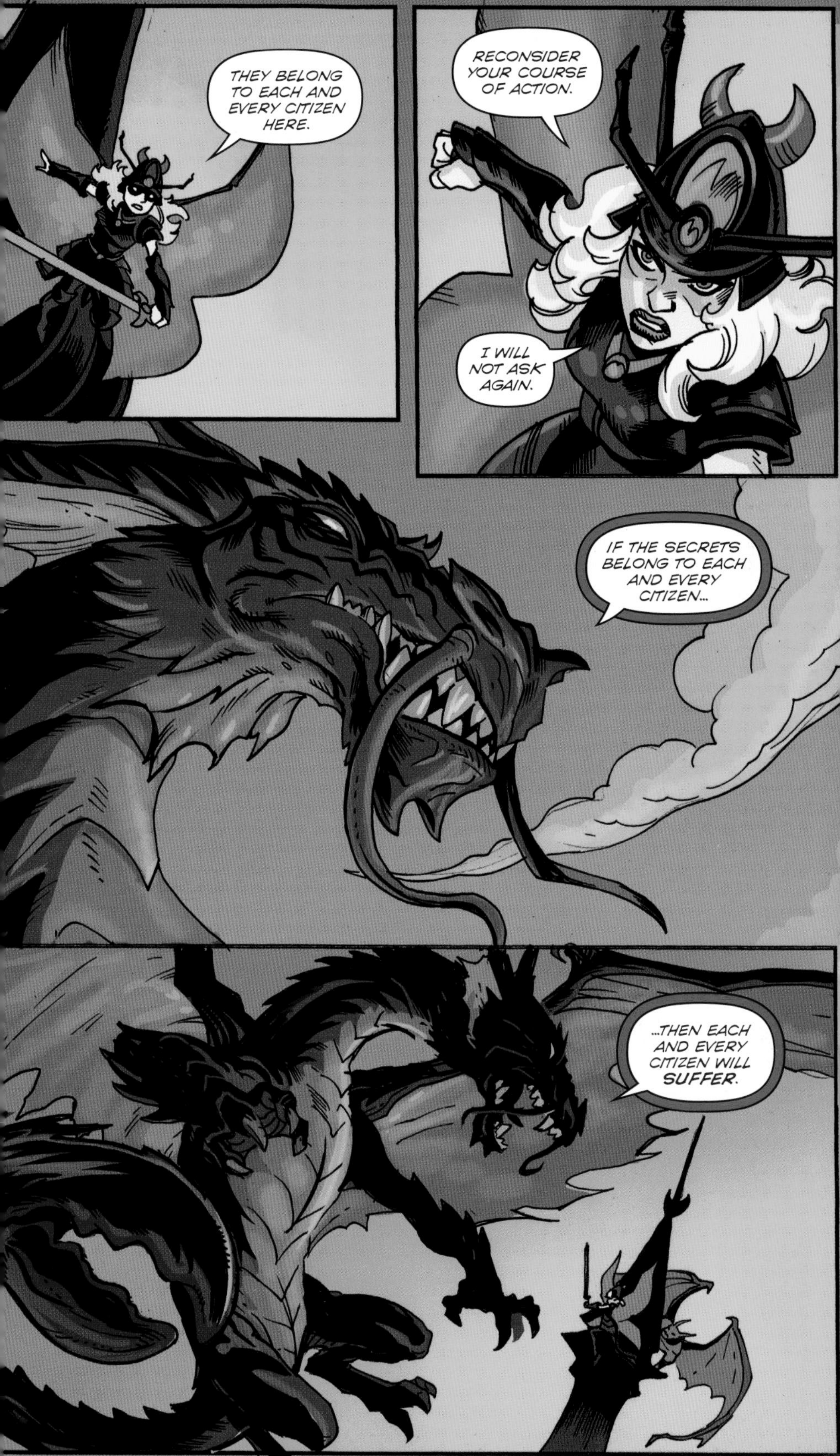
THEY BELONG TO EACH AND EVERY CITIZEN HERE.
RECONSIDER YOUR COURSE OF ACTION.
I WILL NOT ASK AGAIN.
IF THE SECRETS BELONG TO EACH AND EVERY CITIZEN...
...THEN EACH AND EVERY CITIZEN WILL SUFFER.

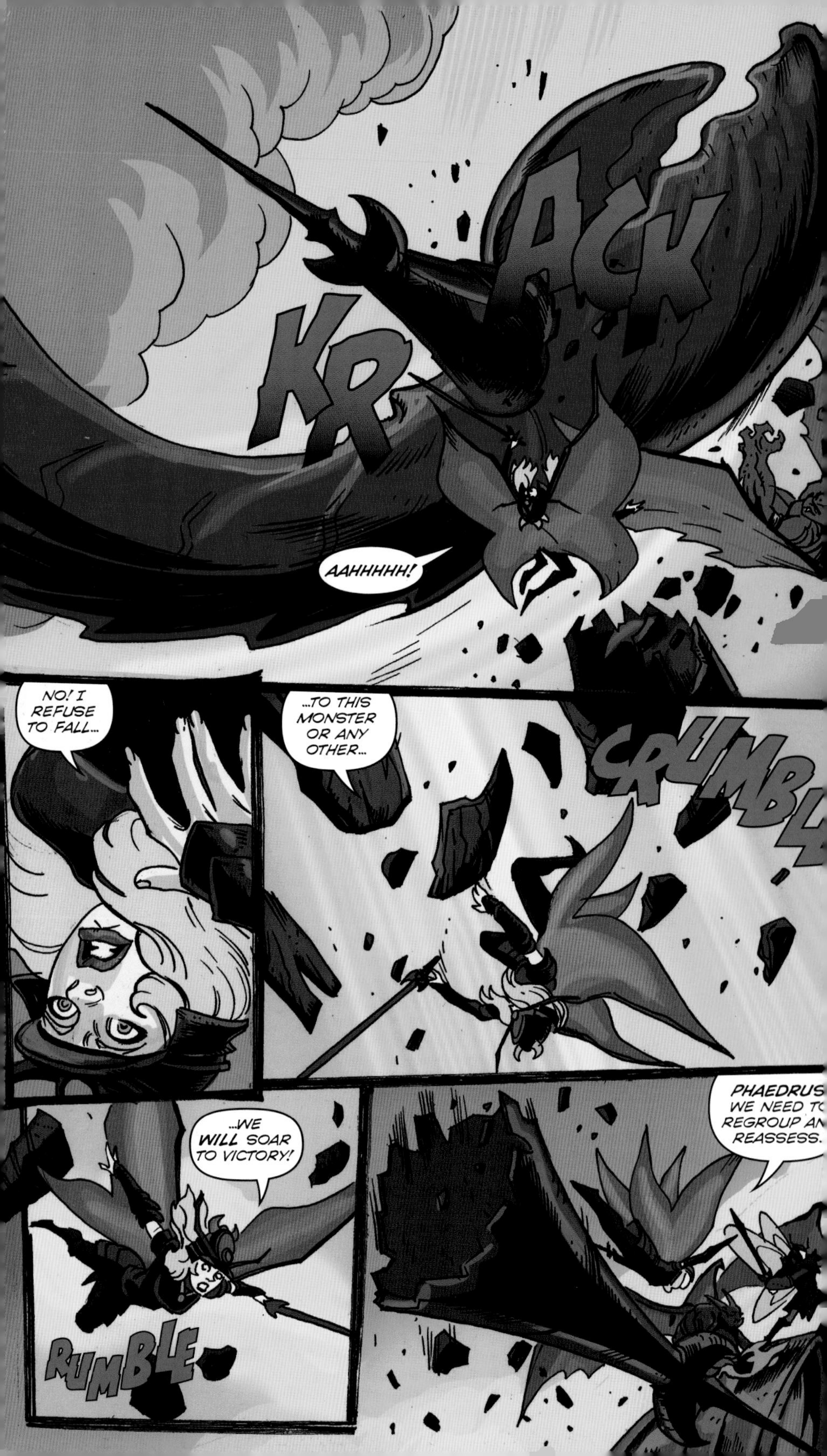
KRACK
AAHHHHH!
NO! I REFUSE TO FALL...
...TO THIS MONSTER OR ANY OTHER...
CRUMBLE
...WE WILL SOAR TO VICTORY!
RUMBLE
PHAEDRUS WE NEED TO REGROUP AN REASSESS.

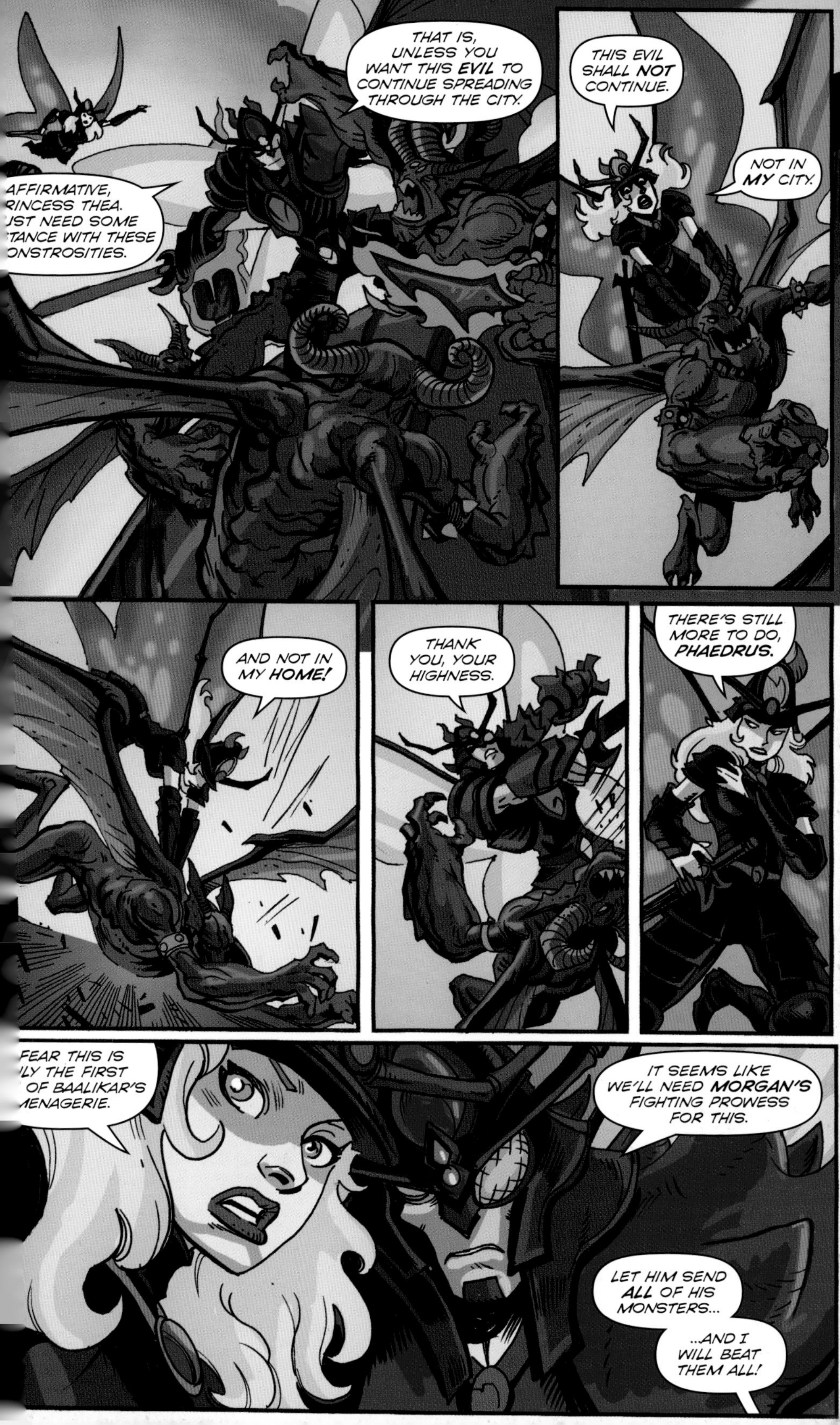
THAT IS, UNLESS YOU WANT THIS EVIL TO CONTINUE SPREADING THROUGH THE CITY.
AFFIRMATIVE, RINCESS THEA. UST NEED SOME TANCE WITH THESE ONSTROSITIES.
THIS EVIL SHALL NOT CONTINUE.
NOT IN MY CITY.
AND NOT IN MY HOME!
THANK YOU, YOUR HIGHNESS.
THERE'S STILL MORE TO DO, PHAEDRUS.
FEAR THIS IS LY THE FIRST OF BAALIKAR'S MENAGERIE.
IT SEEMS LIKE WE'LL NEED MORGAN'S FIGHTING PROWESS FOR THIS.
LET HIM SEND ALL OF HIS MONSTERS...
...AND I WILL BEAT THEM ALL!

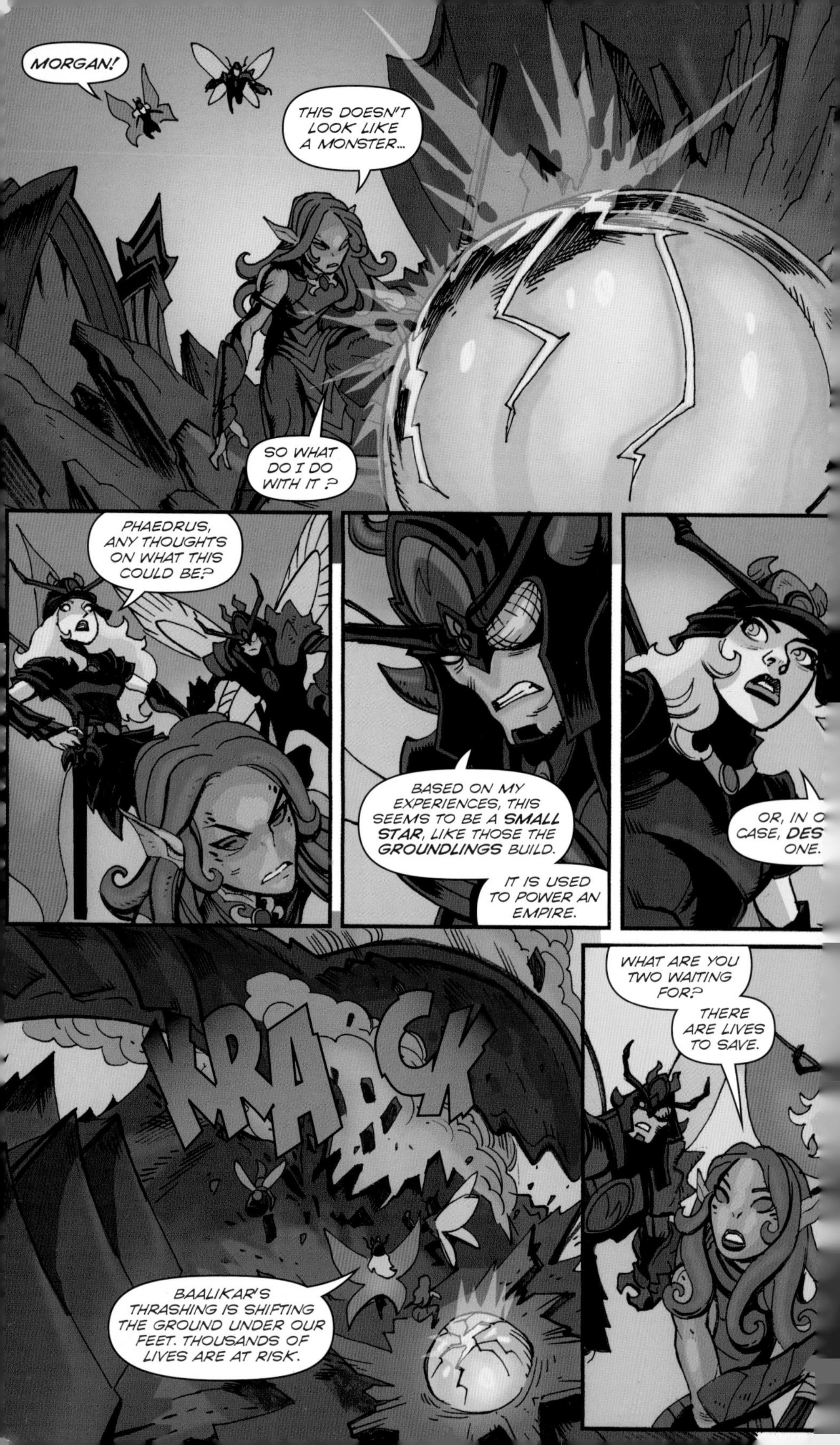
MORGAN!
THIS DOESN'T LOOK LIKE A MONSTER...
SO WHAT DO I DO WITH IT ?
PHAEDRUS, ANY THOUGHTS ON WHAT THIS COULD BE?
BASED ON MY EXPERIENCES, THIS SEEMS TO BE A **SMALL STAR**, LIKE THOSE THE **GROUNDLINGS** BUILD.
IT IS USED TO POWER AN EMPIRE.
OR, IN O
CASE, **DES**
ONE.
KRA-ACK
BAALIKAR'S THRASHING IS SHIFTING THE GROUND UNDER OUR FEET. THOUSANDS OF LIVES ARE AT RISK.
WHAT ARE YOU TWO WAITING FOR?
THERE ARE LIVES TO SAVE.

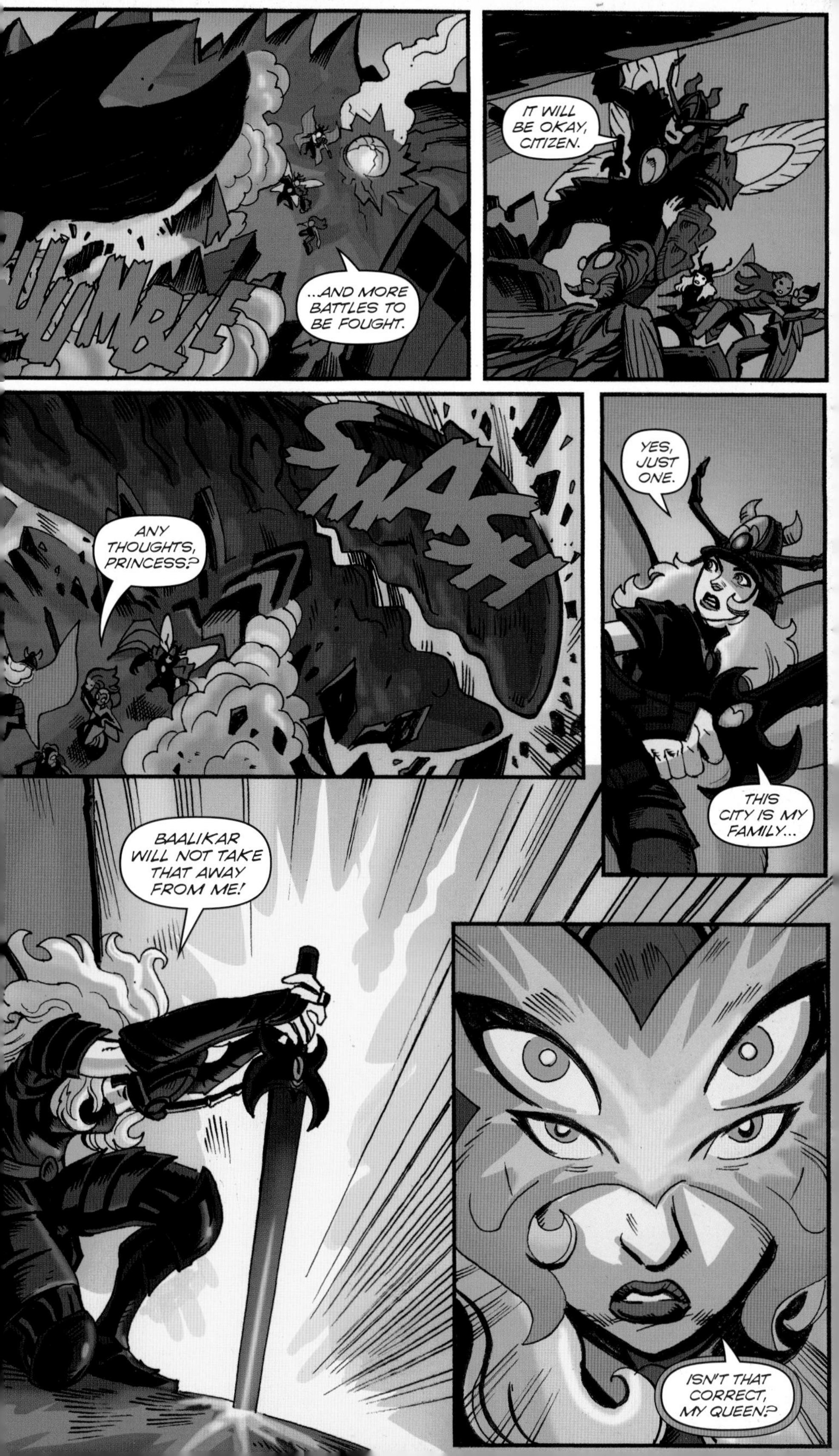
RUMBLE
...AND MORE BATTLES TO BE FOUGHT.
IT WILL BE OKAY, CITIZEN.
SMASH
ANY THOUGHTS, PRINCESS?
YES, JUST ONE.
THIS CITY IS MY FAMILY...
BAALIKAR WILL NOT TAKE THAT AWAY FROM ME!
ISN'T THAT CORRECT, MY QUEEN?

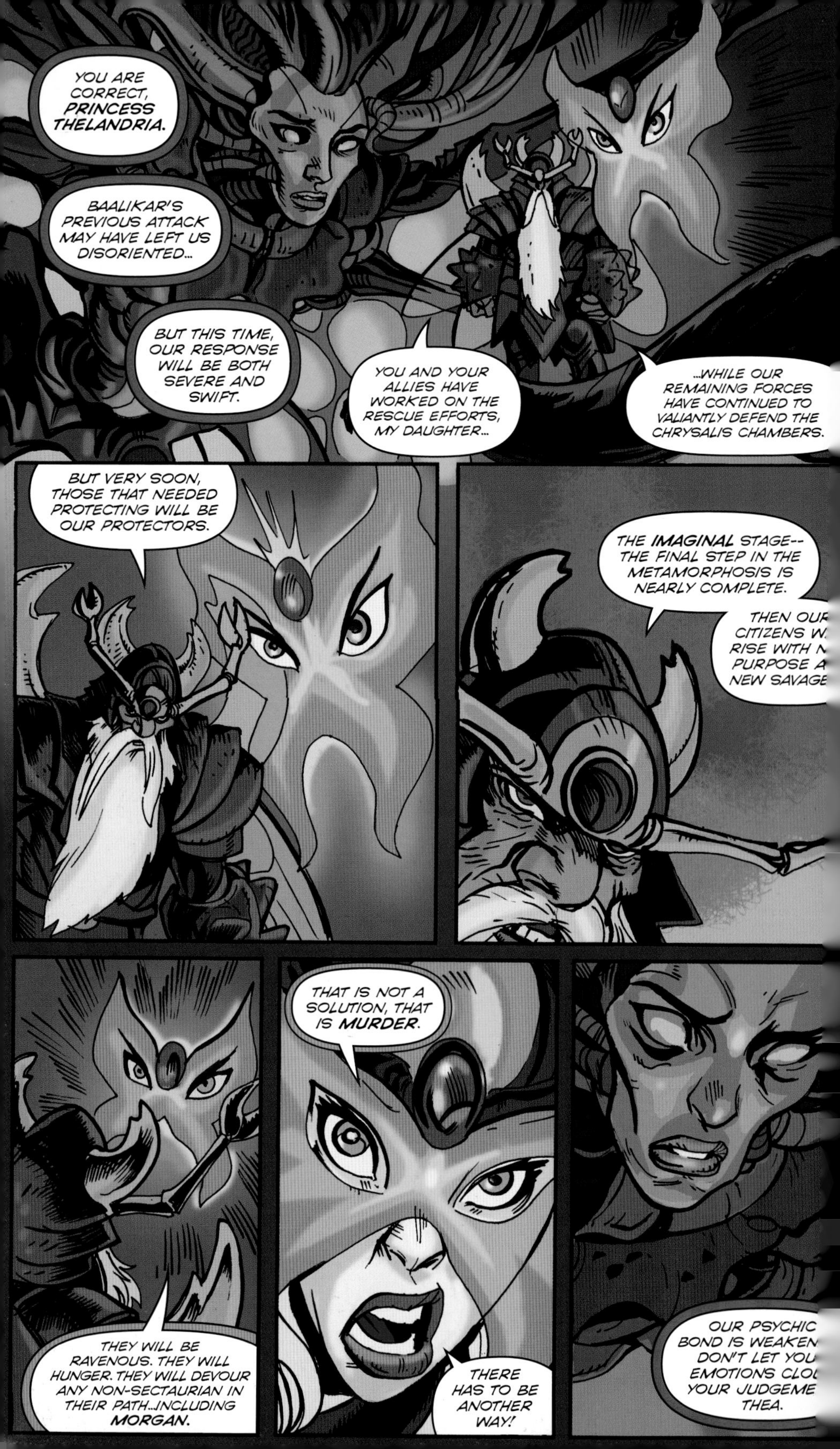
YOU ARE CORRECT, **PRINCESS THELANDRIA.**
BAALIKAR'S PREVIOUS ATTACK MAY HAVE LEFT US DISORIENTED...
BUT THIS TIME, OUR RESPONSE WILL BE BOTH SEVERE AND SWIFT.
YOU AND YOUR ALLIES HAVE WORKED ON THE RESCUE EFFORTS, MY DAUGHTER...
...WHILE OUR REMAINING FORCES HAVE CONTINUED TO VALIANTLY DEFEND THE CHRYSALIS CHAMBERS.
BUT VERY SOON, THOSE THAT NEEDED PROTECTING WILL BE OUR PROTECTORS.
THE **IMAGINAL** STAGE-- THE FINAL STEP IN THE METAMORPHOSIS IS NEARLY COMPLETE.
THEN OU CITIZENS W RISE WITH PURPOSE NEW SAVAGE
THEY WILL BE RAVENOUS. THEY WILL HUNGER. THEY WILL DEVOUR ANY NON-SECTAURIAN IN THEIR PATH...INCLUDING **MORGAN.**
THAT IS NOT A SOLUTION, THAT IS **MURDER.**
THERE HAS TO BE ANOTHER WAY!
OUR PSYCHIC BOND IS WEAKEN DON'T LET YOU EMOTIONS CLO YOUR JUDGEME THEA.

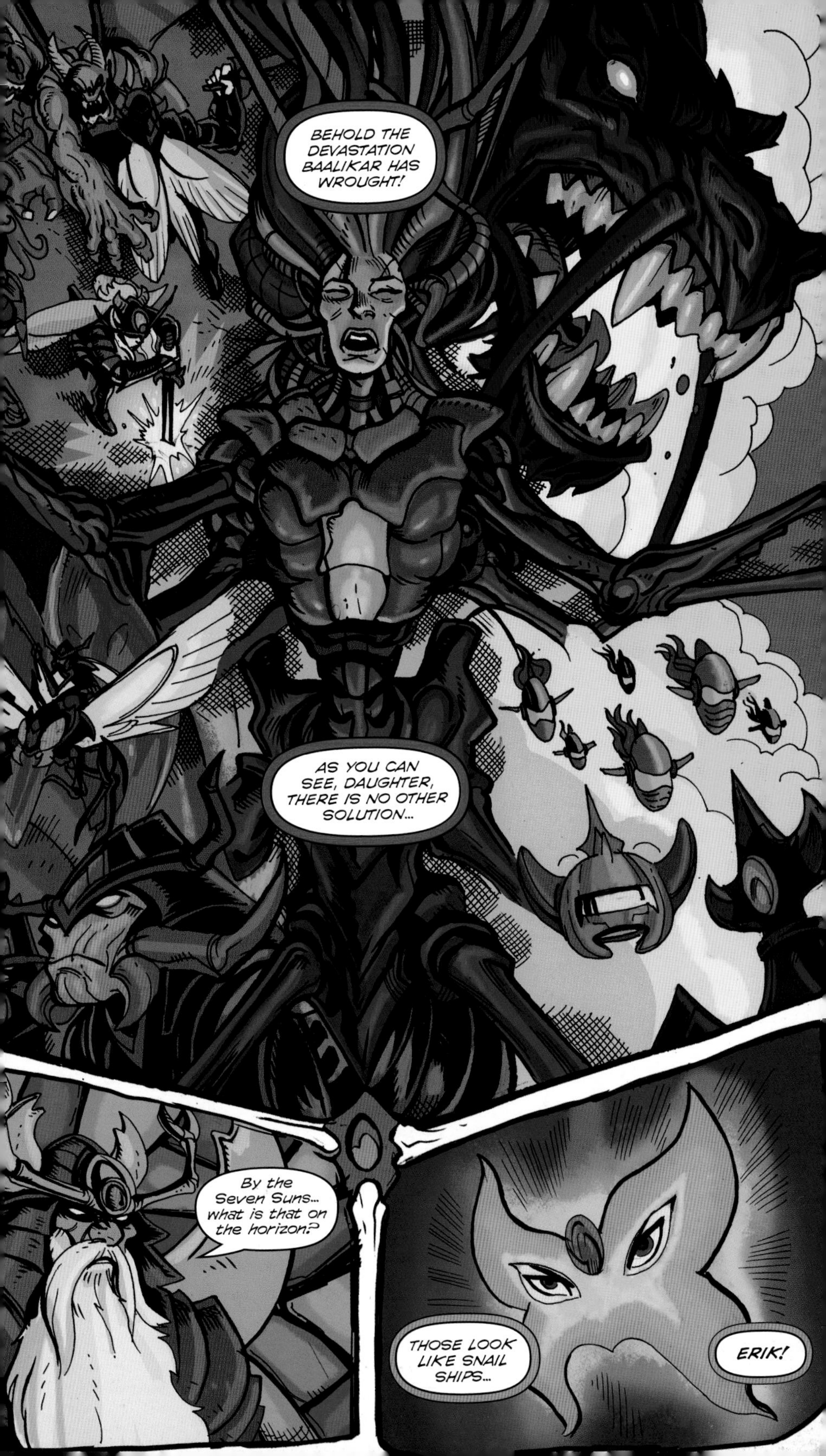
BEHOLD THE DEVASTATION BAALIKAR HAS WROUGHT!
AS YOU CAN SEE, DAUGHTER, THERE IS NO OTHER SOLUTION...
By the Seven Suns... what is that on the horizon?
THOSE LOOK LIKE SNAIL SHIPS...
ERIK!

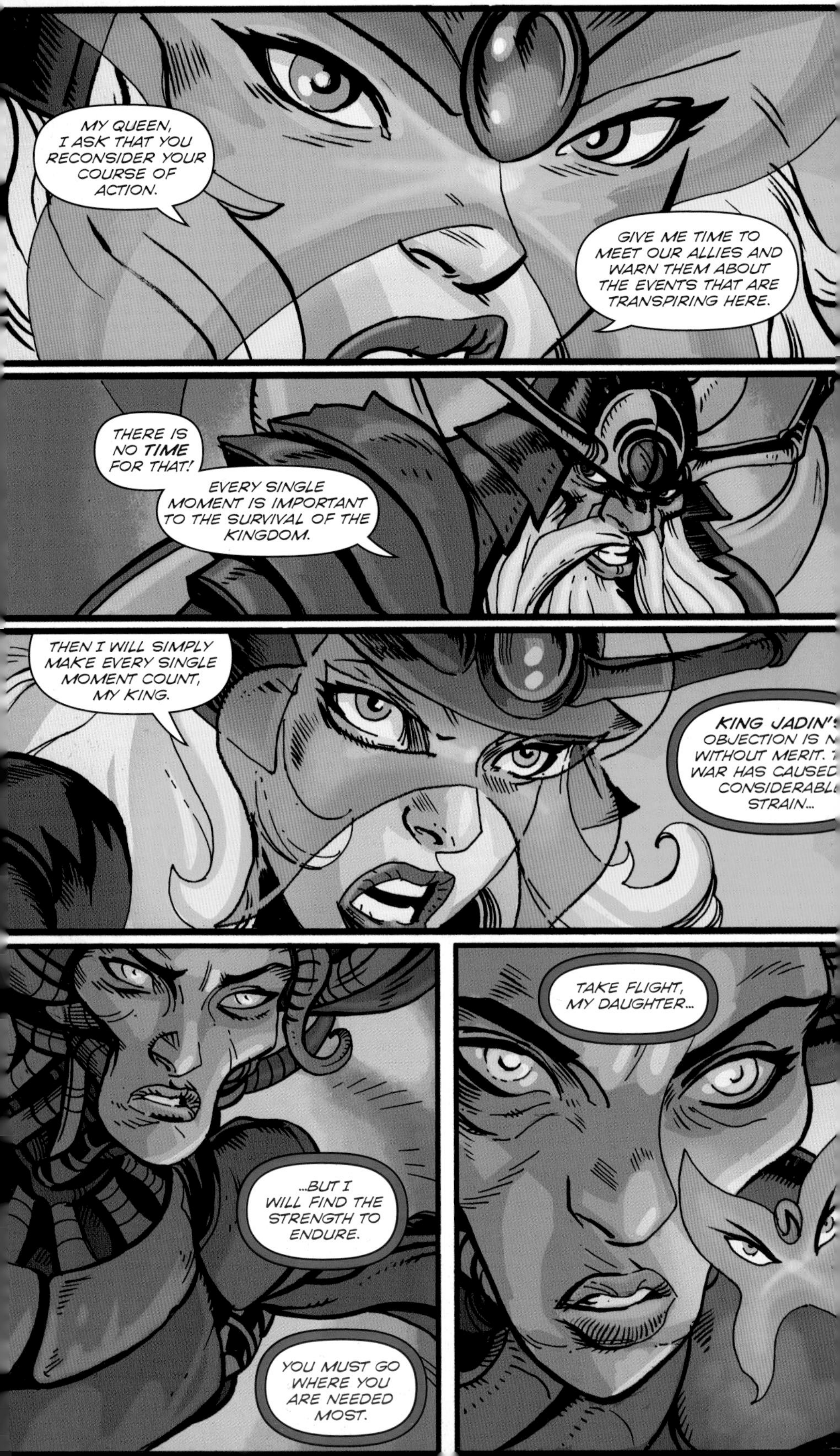
MY QUEEN, I ASK THAT YOU RECONSIDER YOUR COURSE OF ACTION.
GIVE ME TIME TO MEET OUR ALLIES AND WARN THEM ABOUT THE EVENTS THAT ARE TRANSPIRING HERE.
THERE IS NO **TIME** FOR THAT!
EVERY SINGLE MOMENT IS IMPORTANT TO THE SURVIVAL OF THE KINGDOM.
THEN I WILL SIMPLY MAKE EVERY SINGLE MOMENT COUNT, MY KING.
KING JADIN' OBJECTION IS N WITHOUT MERIT. WAR HAS CAUSED CONSIDERABL STRAIN...
...BUT I WILL FIND THE STRENGTH TO ENDURE.
YOU MUST GO WHERE YOU ARE NEEDED MOST.
TAKE FLIGHT, MY DAUGHTER...

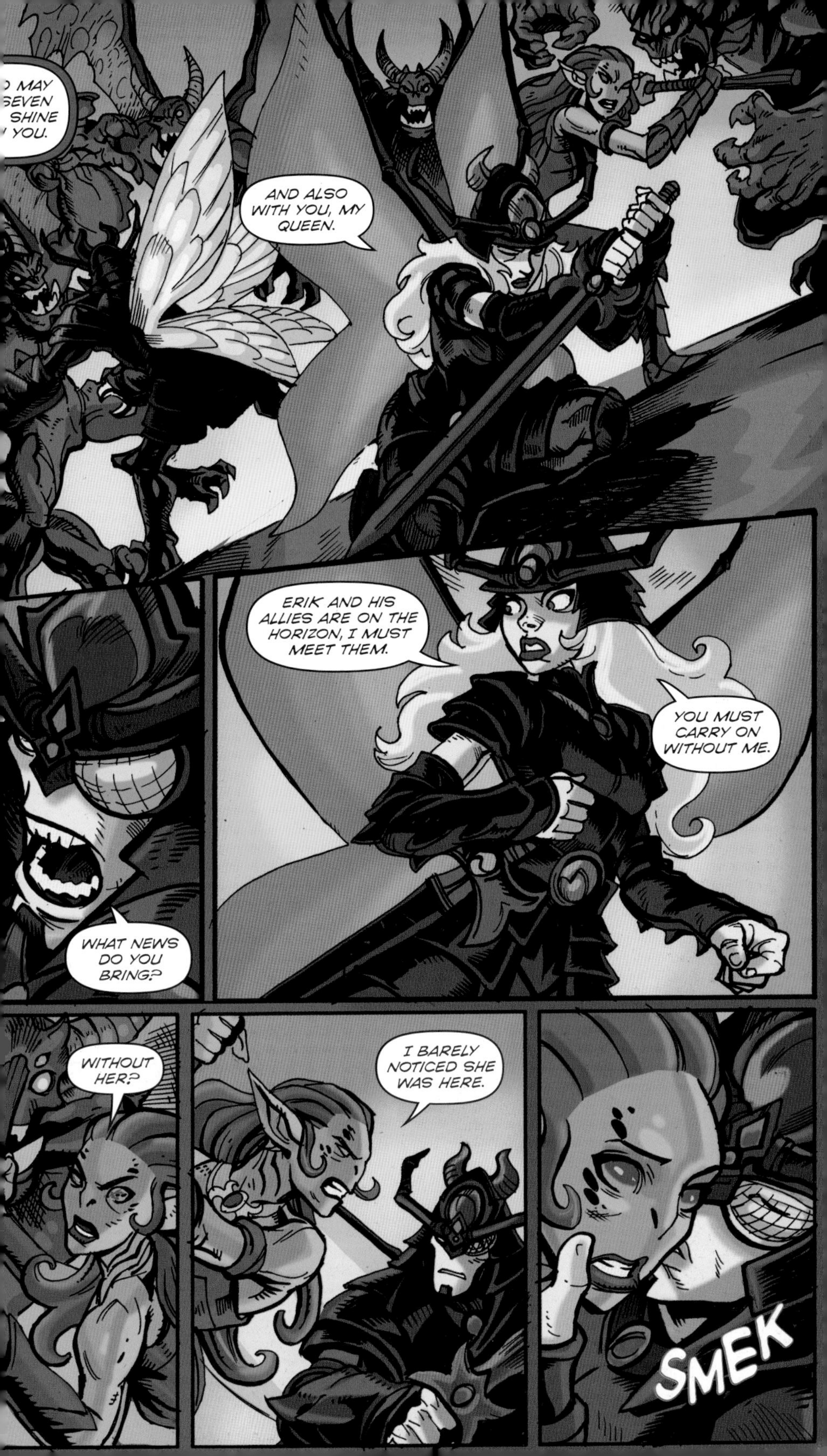

AND ALSO WITH YOU, MY QUEEN.
WHAT NEWS DO YOU BRING?
ERIK AND HIS ALLIES ARE ON THE HORIZON, I MUST MEET THEM.
YOU MUST CARRY ON WITHOUT ME.
WITHOUT HER?
I BARELY NOTICED SHE WAS HERE.
SMEK

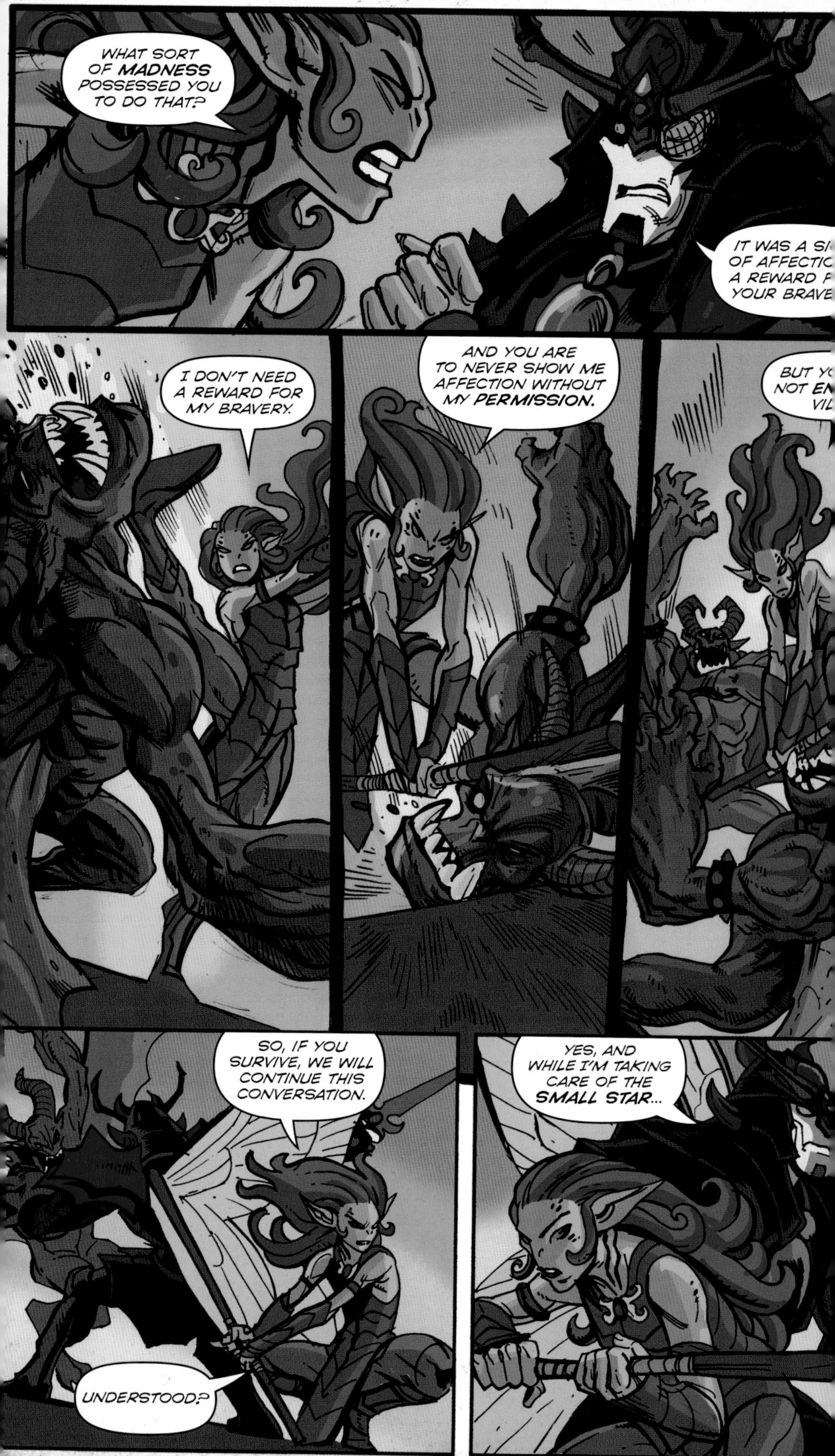
WHAT SORT OF MADNESS POSSESSED YOU TO DO THAT?
IT WAS A SI OF AFFECTIC A REWARD F YOUR BRAVE
I DON'T NEED A REWARD FOR MY BRAVERY.
AND YOU ARE TO NEVER SHOW ME AFFECTION WITHOUT MY PERMISSION.
SO, IF YOU SURVIVE, WE WILL CONTINUE THIS CONVERSATION.
UNDERSTOOD?
YES, AND WHILE I'M TAKING CARE OF THE SMALL STAR...

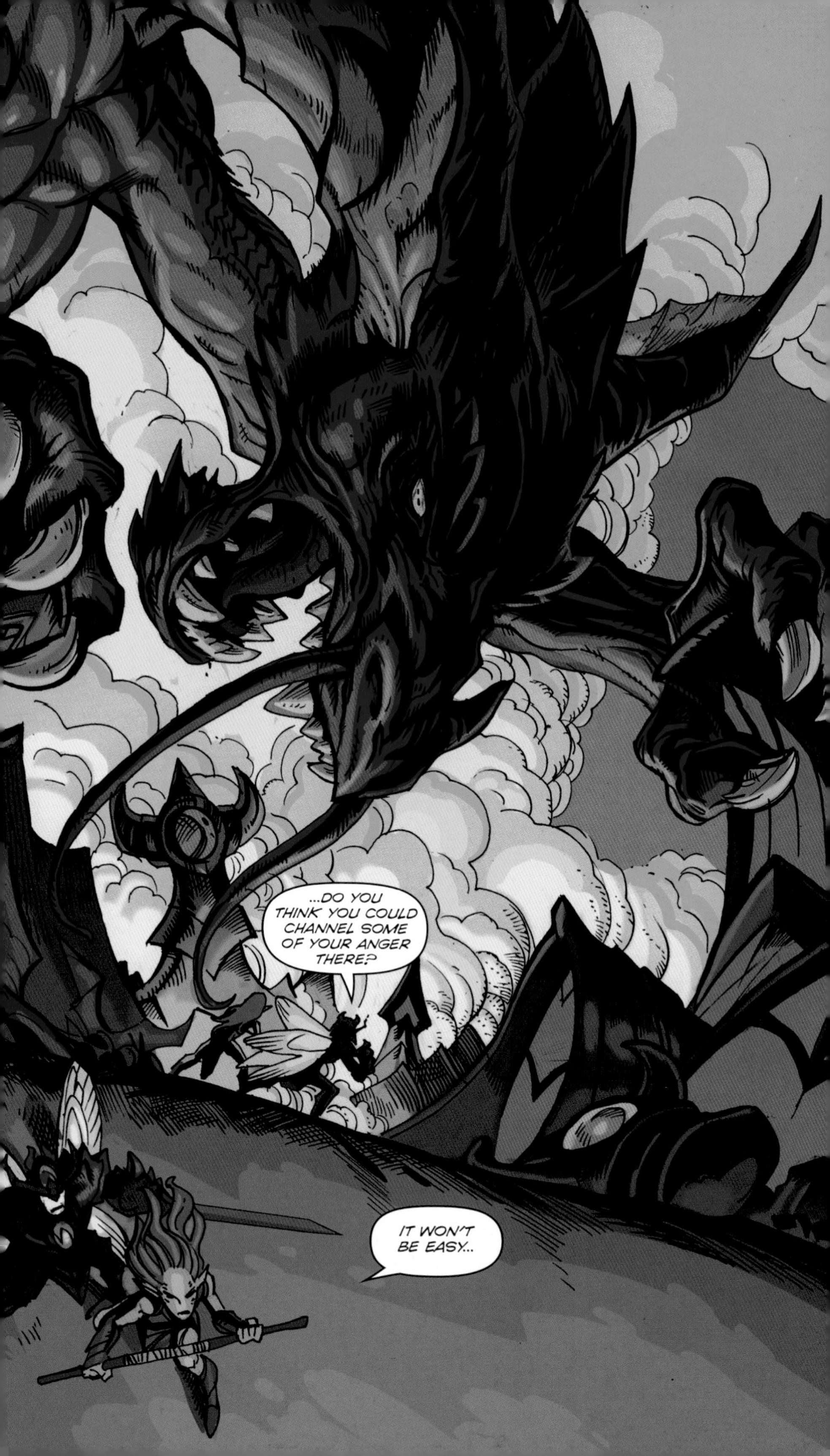
...DO YOU THINK YOU COULD CHANNEL SOME OF YOUR ANGER THERE?
IT WON'T BE EASY...

...BUT IT WILL BE FUN.

WE SHOULD BE APPROACHING THE HIVE CITY SHORTLY.

DO THE REST OF Y SEE THAT

WHA YOU IT

A-KU!

NOTHING TRAVELING THAT FAST COULD POSSIBLY BE FRIENDLY.

I CONCUR, SISTER TESSA. EVADE IT, BOX.

WAIT, RAJ NOD... I THINK--

EVADE!

NO. TRUST ME ON THIS...

IT'S THEA!

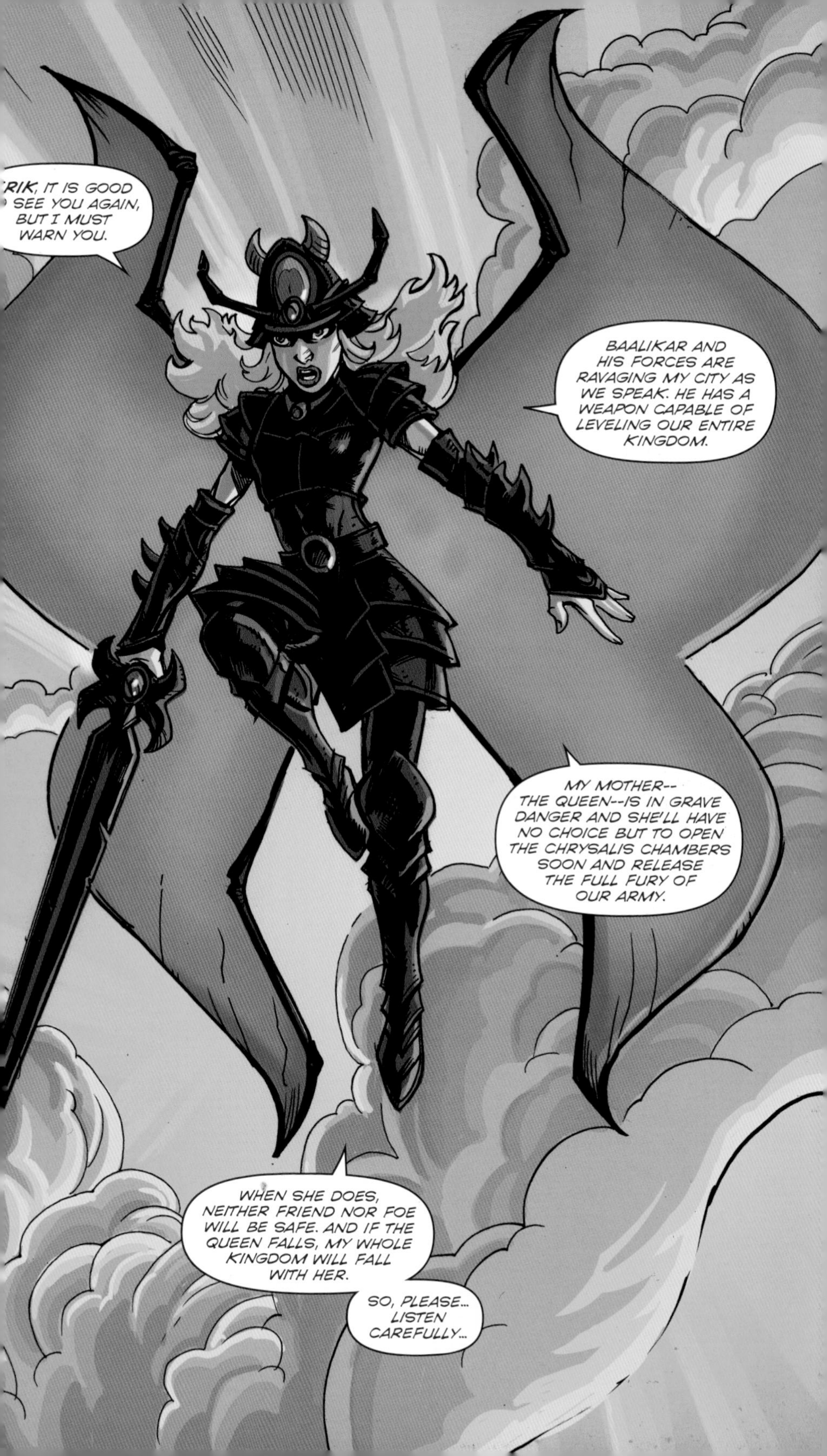
RIK, IT IS GOOD
SEE YOU AGAIN, BUT I MUST WARN YOU.
BAALIKAR AND HIS FORCES ARE RAVAGING MY CITY AS WE SPEAK. HE HAS A WEAPON CAPABLE OF LEVELING OUR ENTIRE KINGDOM.
MY MOTHER-- THE QUEEN--IS IN GRAVE DANGER AND SHE'LL HAVE NO CHOICE BUT TO OPEN THE CHRYSALIS CHAMBERS SOON AND RELEASE THE FULL FURY OF OUR ARMY.
WHEN SHE DOES, NEITHER FRIEND NOR FOE WILL BE SAFE. AND IF THE QUEEN FALLS, MY WHOLE KINGDOM WILL FALL WITH HER.
SO, PLEASE... LISTEN CAREFULLY...

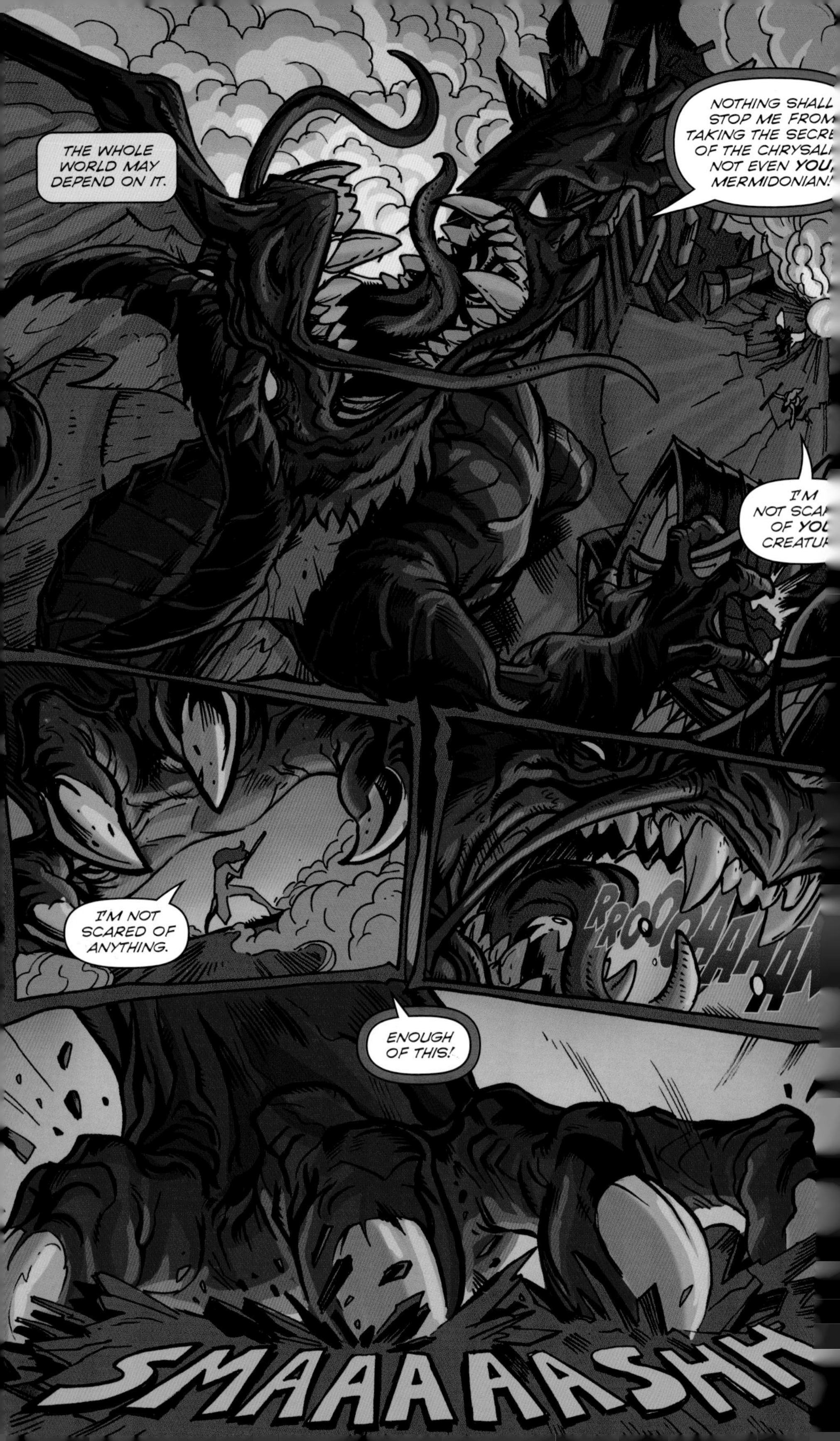
THE WHOLE WORLD MAY DEPEND ON IT.
NOTHING SHALL STOP ME FROM TAKING THE SECRE OF THE CHRYSALI NOT EVEN YOU, MERMIDONIAN!
I'M NOT SCA OF YOU CREATU
I'M NOT SCARED OF ANYTHING.
RROOOAAAH
ENOUGH OF THIS!
SMAAAAASH

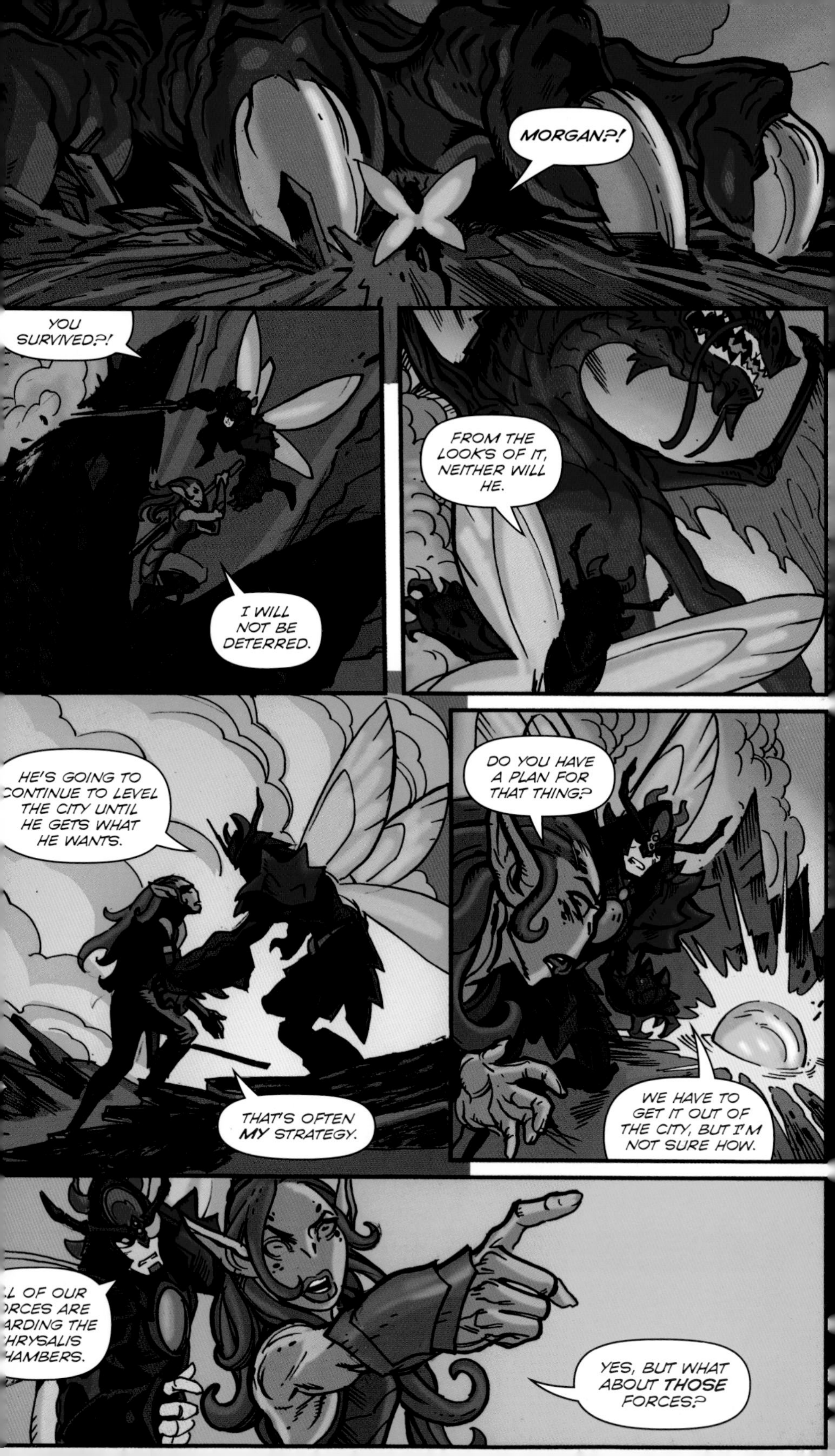
MORGAN?!
YOU SURVIVED?!
I WILL NOT BE DETERRED.
FROM THE LOOKS OF IT, NEITHER WILL HE.
HE'S GOING TO CONTINUE TO LEVEL THE CITY UNTIL HE GETS WHAT HE WANTS.
THAT'S OFTEN MY STRATEGY.
DO YOU HAVE A PLAN FOR THAT THING?
WE HAVE TO GET IT OUT OF THE CITY, BUT I'M NOT SURE HOW.
YES, BUT WHAT ABOUT THOSE FORCES?

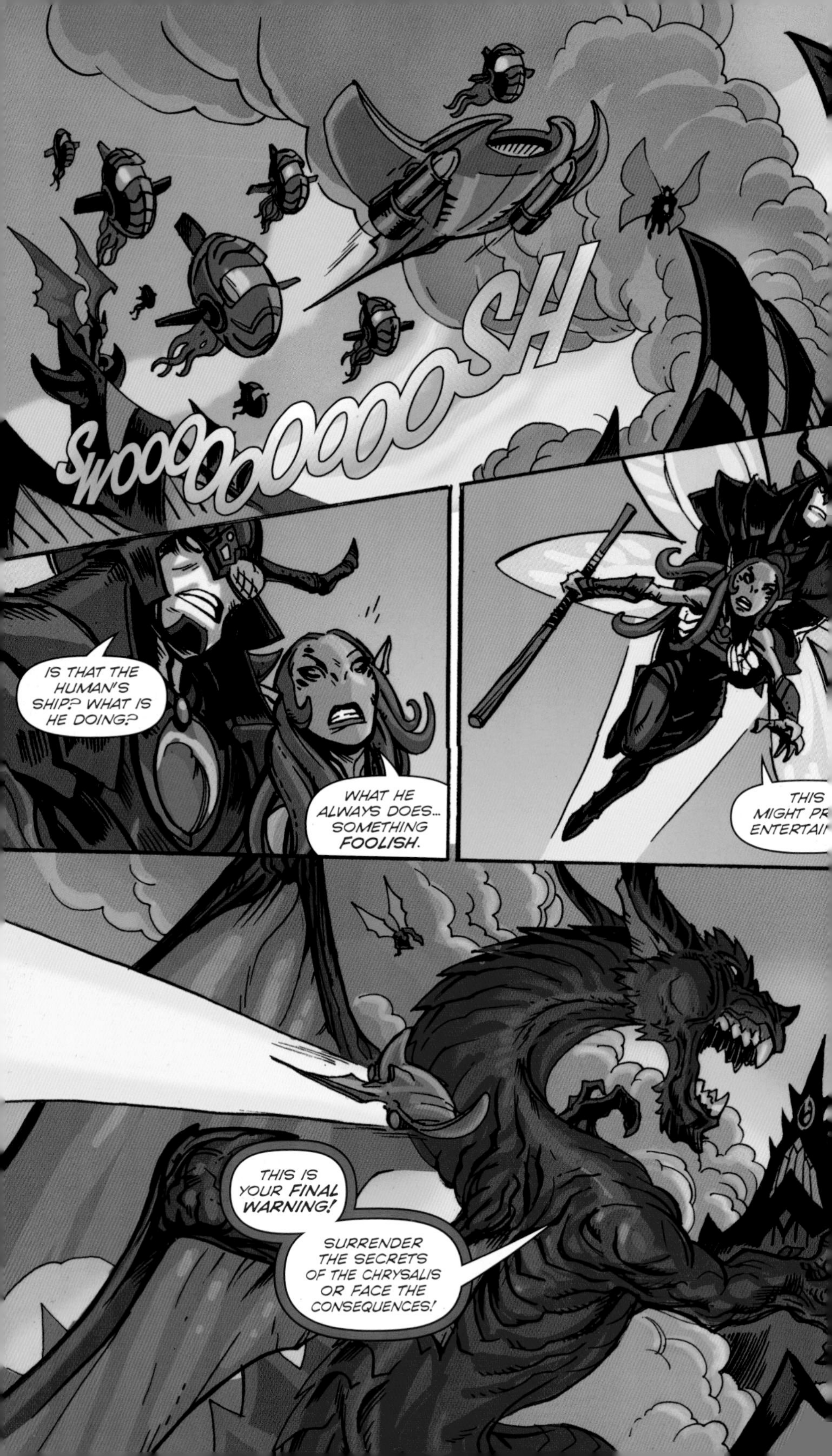
SWOOOOOOOOOSH
IS THAT THE HUMAN'S SHIP? WHAT IS HE DOING?
WHAT HE ALWAYS DOES... SOMETHING FOOLISH.
THIS MIGHT PR ENTERTAI
THIS IS YOUR FINAL WARNING!
SURRENDER THE SECRETS OF THE CHRYSALIS OR FACE THE CONSEQUENCES!

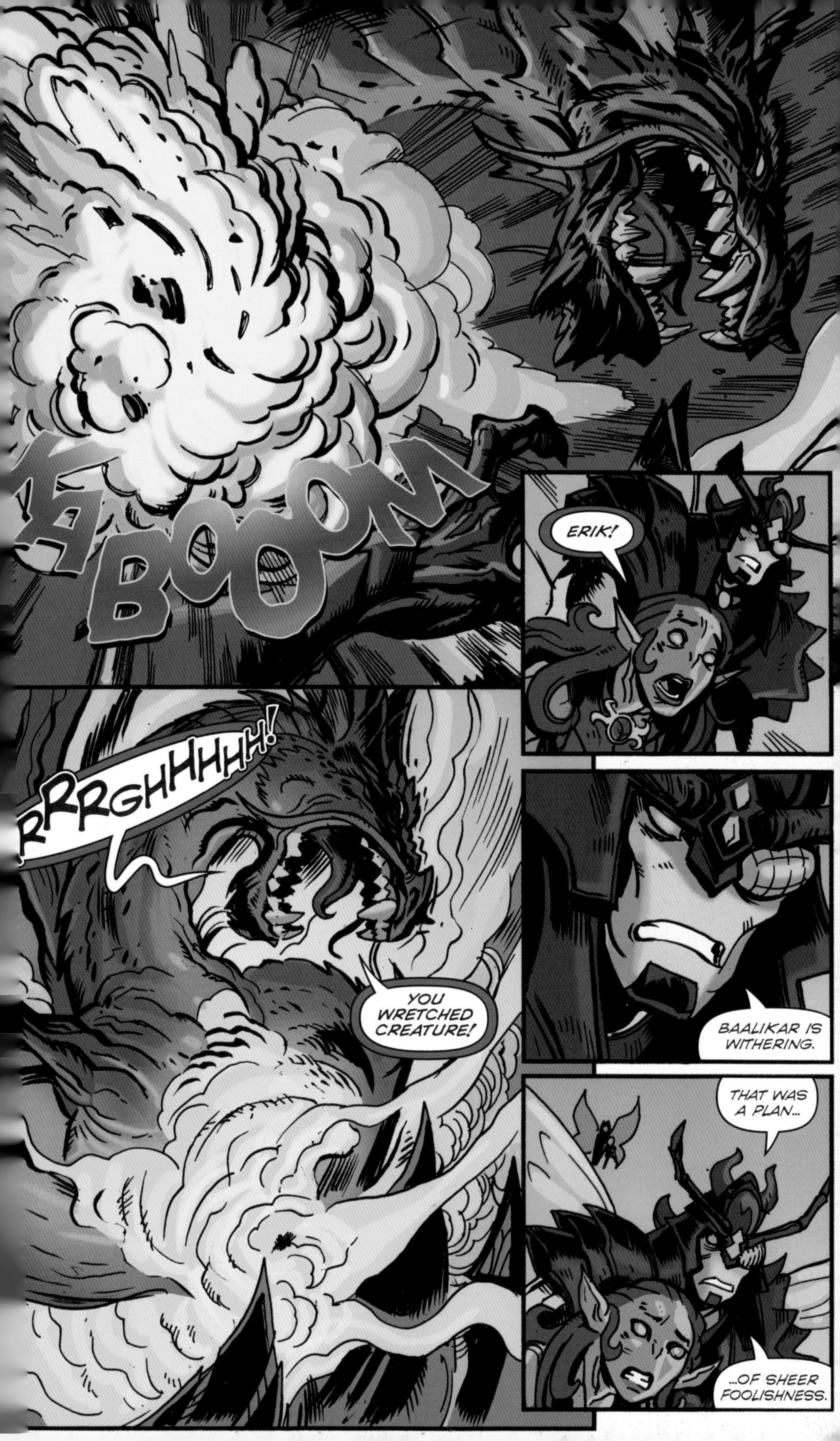

KABOOOM
ERIK!
RRRGHHHHH!
YOU WRETCHED CREATURE!
BAALIKAR IS WITHERING.
THAT WAS A PLAN...
...OF SHEER FOOLISHNESS.

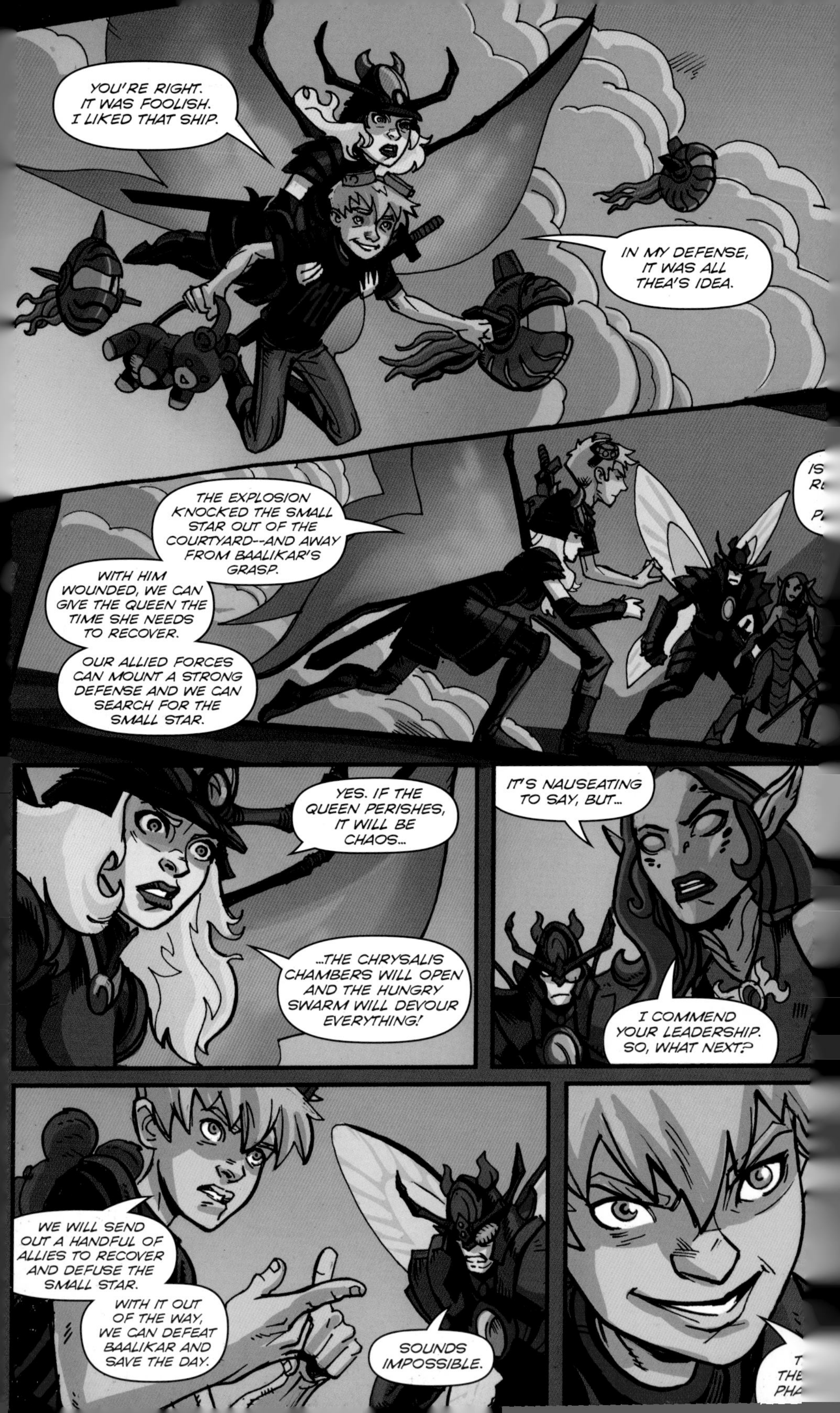

YOU'RE RIGHT. IT WAS FOOLISH. I LIKED THAT SHIP.
IN MY DEFENSE, IT WAS ALL THEA'S IDEA.
THE EXPLOSION KNOCKED THE SMALL STAR OUT OF THE COURTYARD--AND AWAY FROM BAALIKAR'S GRASP.
WITH HIM WOUNDED, WE CAN GIVE THE QUEEN THE TIME SHE NEEDS TO RECOVER.
OUR ALLIED FORCES CAN MOUNT A STRONG DEFENSE AND WE CAN SEARCH FOR THE SMALL STAR.
YES. IF THE QUEEN PERISHES, IT WILL BE CHAOS...
...THE CHRYSALIS CHAMBERS WILL OPEN AND THE HUNGRY SWARM WILL DEVOUR EVERYTHING!
IT'S NAUSEATING TO SAY, BUT...
I COMMEND YOUR LEADERSHIP. SO, WHAT NEXT?
WE WILL SEND OUT A HANDFUL OF ALLIES TO RECOVER AND DEFUSE THE SMALL STAR.
WITH IT OUT OF THE WAY, WE CAN DEFEAT BAALIKAR AND SAVE THE DAY.
SOUNDS IMPOSSIBLE.

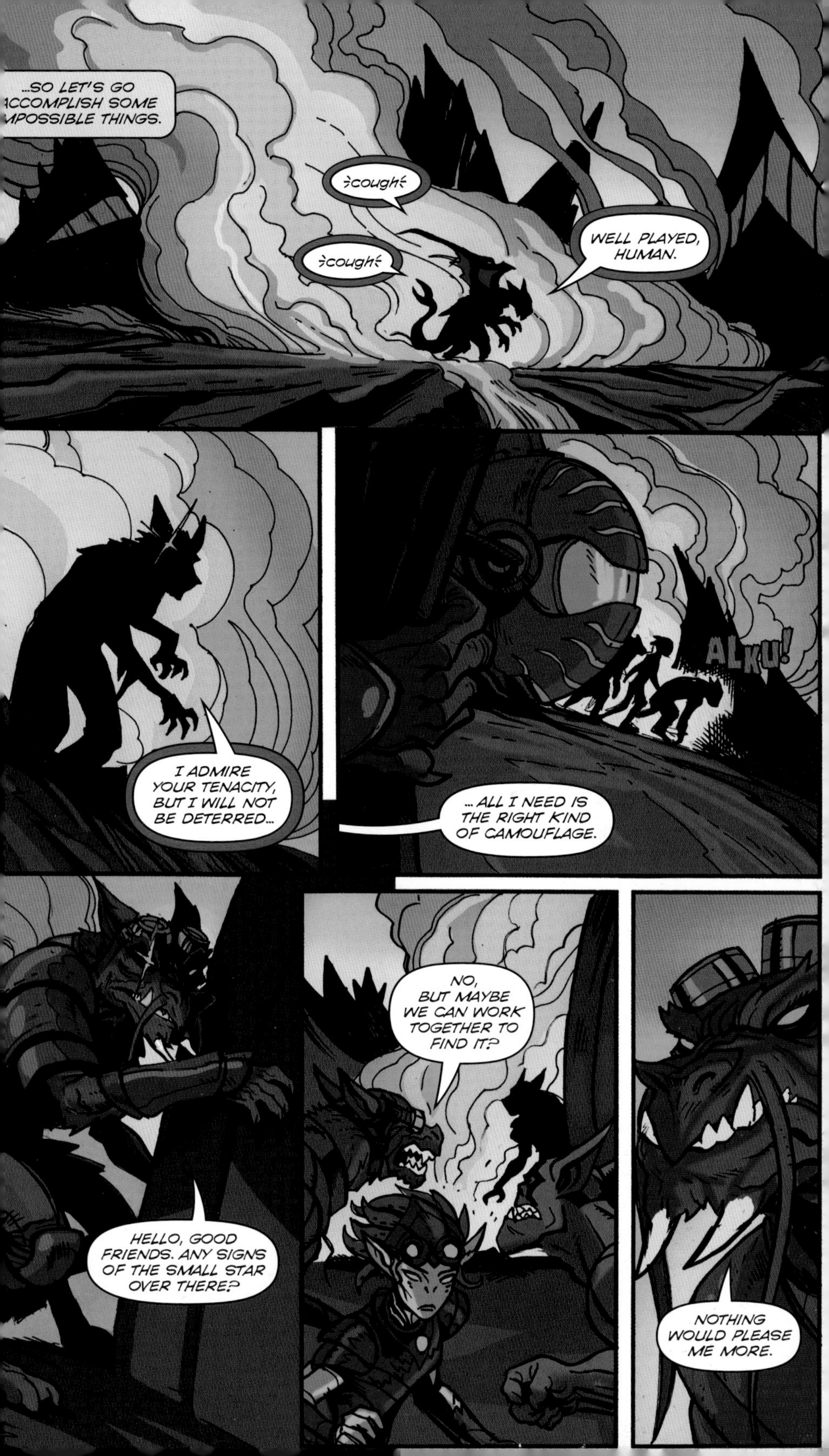

...SO LET'S GO ACCOMPLISH SOME IMPOSSIBLE THINGS.
>cough<
>cough<
WELL PLAYED, HUMAN.
I ADMIRE YOUR TENACITY, BUT I WILL NOT BE DETERRED...
...ALL I NEED IS THE RIGHT KIND OF CAMOUFLAGE.
ALKU!
HELLO, GOOD FRIENDS. ANY SIGNS OF THE SMALL STAR OVER THERE?
NO, BUT MAYBE WE CAN WORK TOGETHER TO FIND IT?
NOTHING WOULD PLEASE ME MORE.

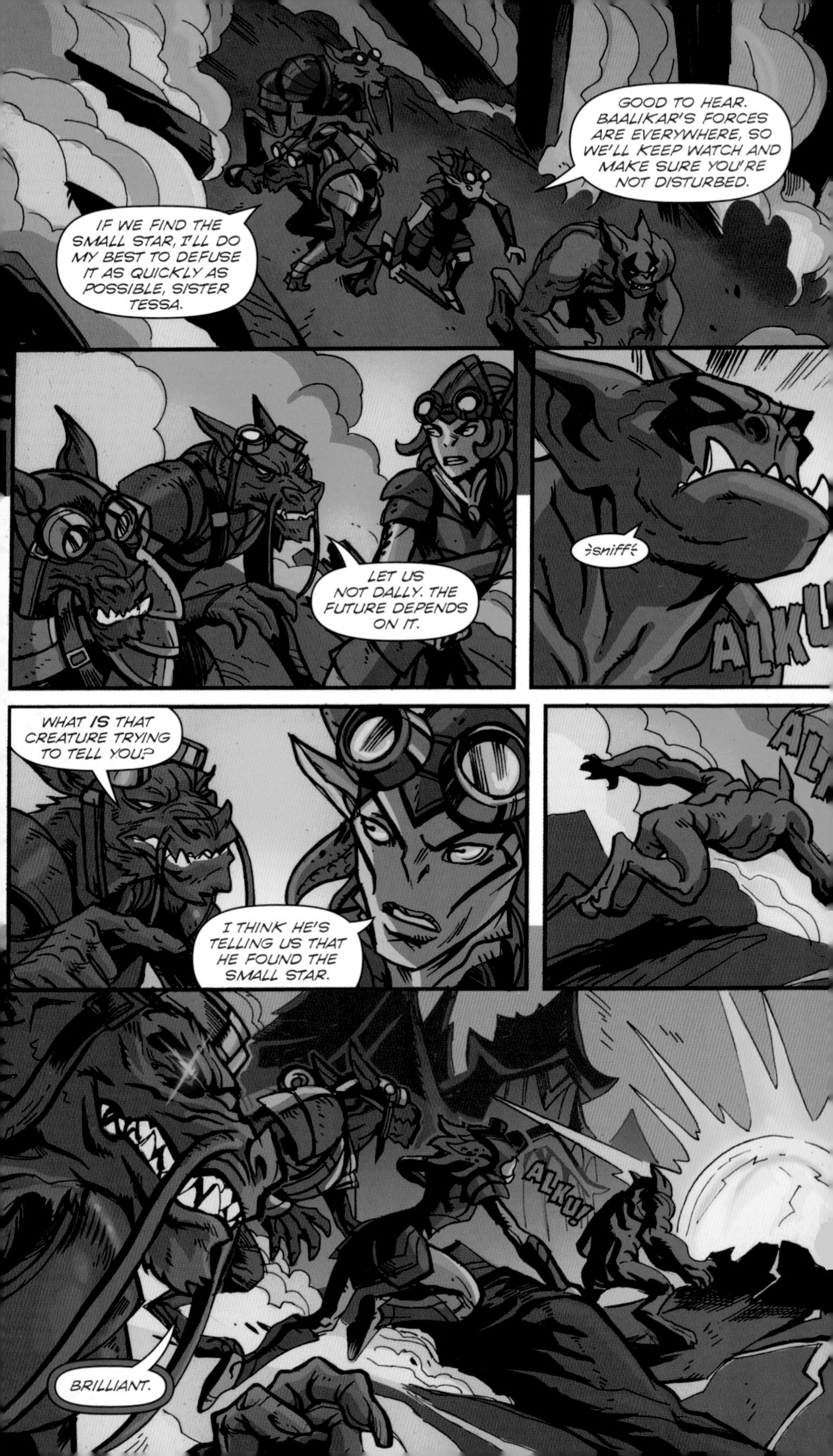
GOOD TO HEAR. BAALIKAR'S FORCES ARE EVERYWHERE, SO WE'LL KEEP WATCH AND MAKE SURE YOU'RE NOT DISTURBED.
IF WE FIND THE SMALL STAR, I'LL DO MY BEST TO DEFUSE IT AS QUICKLY AS POSSIBLE, SISTER TESSA.
LET US NOT DALLY. THE FUTURE DEPENDS ON IT.
sniff
ALKU
WHAT IS THAT CREATURE TRYING TO TELL YOU?
I THINK HE'S TELLING US THAT HE FOUND THE SMALL STAR.
ALKU!
BRILLIANT.

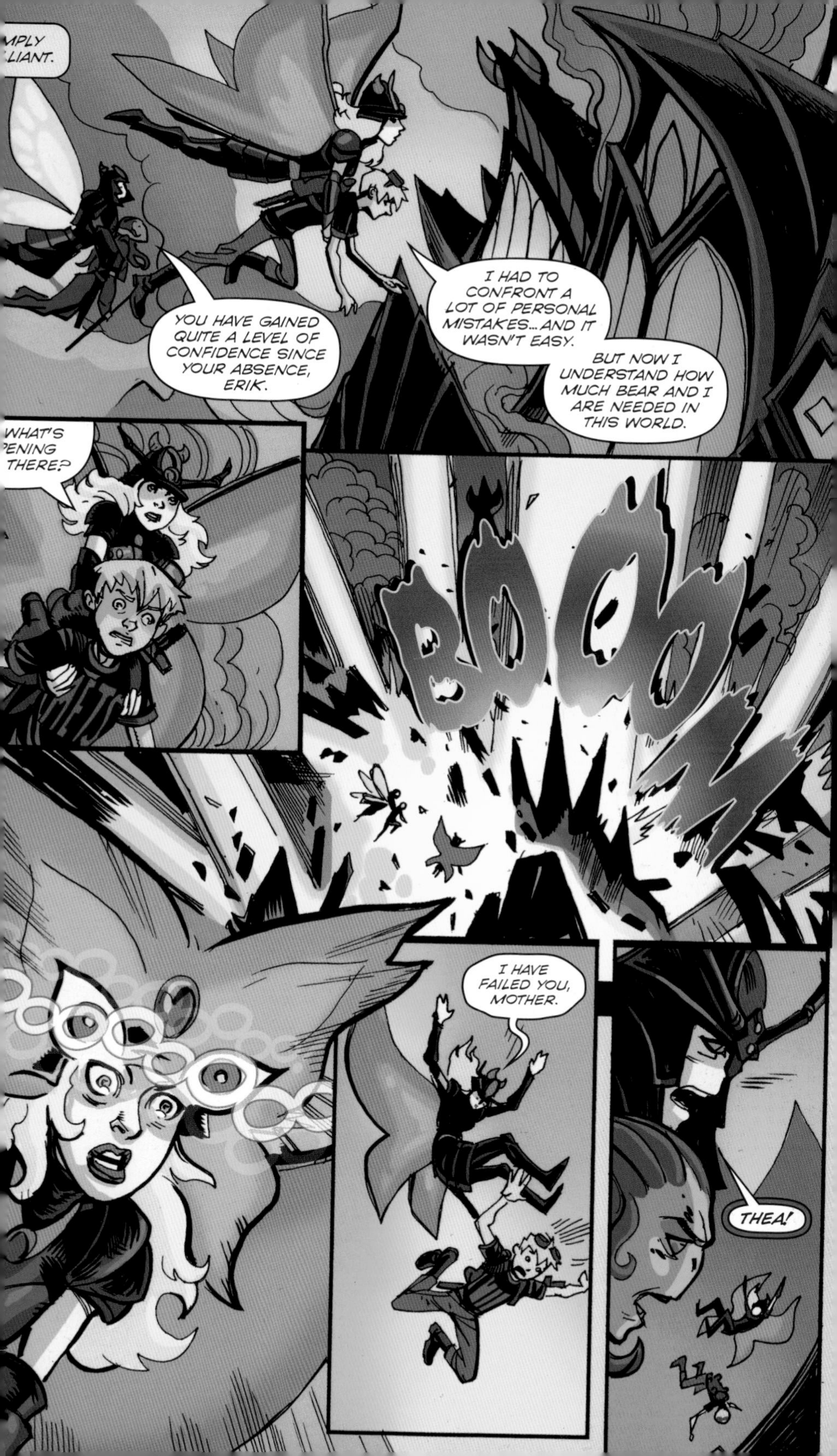
MPLY
LIANT.
YOU HAVE GAINED QUITE A LEVEL OF CONFIDENCE SINCE YOUR ABSENCE, ERIK.
I HAD TO CONFRONT A LOT OF PERSONAL MISTAKES... AND IT WASN'T EASY.
BUT NOW I UNDERSTAND HOW MUCH BEAR AND I ARE NEEDED IN THIS WORLD.
WHAT'S
PENING
THERE?
BOOOM
I HAVE FAILED YOU, MOTHER.
THEA!

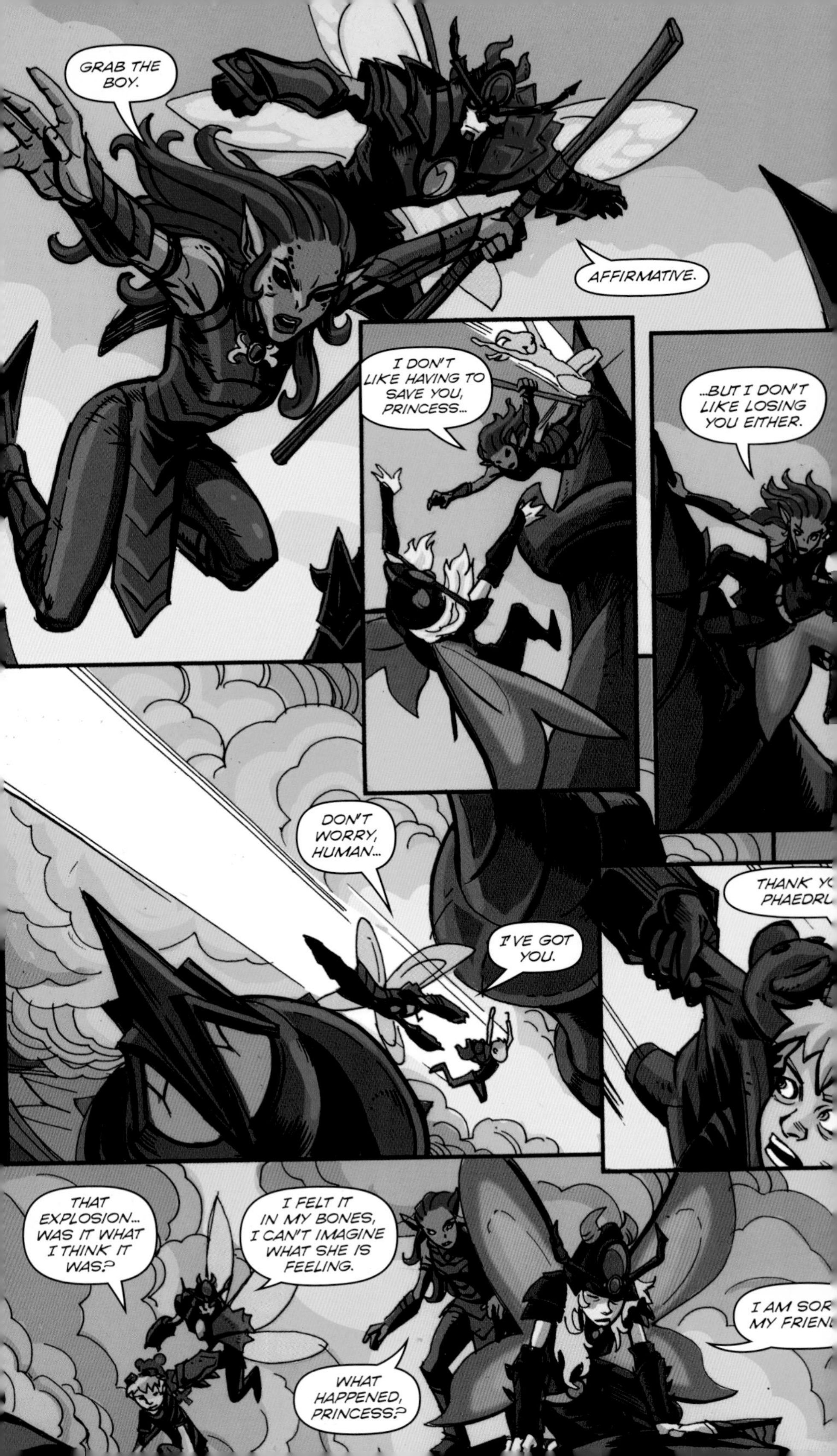
GRAB THE BOY.
AFFIRMATIVE.
I DON'T LIKE HAVING TO SAVE YOU, PRINCESS...
...BUT I DON'T LIKE LOSING YOU EITHER.
DON'T WORRY, HUMAN...
I'VE GOT YOU.
THANK YO PHAEDRU
THAT EXPLOSION... WAS IT WHAT I THINK IT WAS?
I FELT IT IN MY BONES, I CAN'T IMAGINE WHAT SHE IS FEELING.
WHAT HAPPENED, PRINCESS?
I AM SOR MY FRIEN

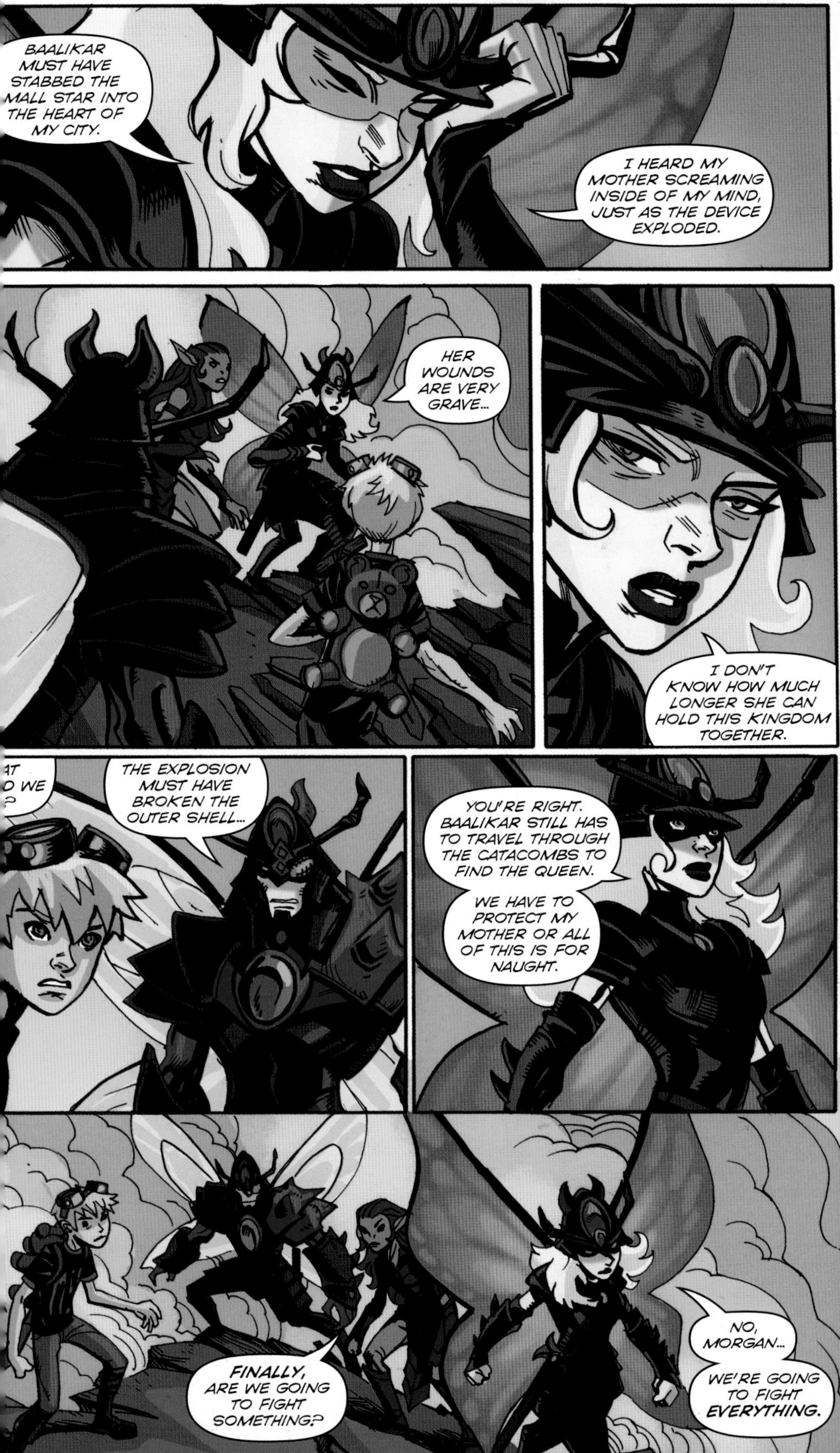
BAALIKAR MUST HAVE STABBED THE MALL STAR INTO THE HEART OF MY CITY.
I HEARD MY MOTHER SCREAMING INSIDE OF MY MIND, JUST AS THE DEVICE EXPLODED.
HER WOUNDS ARE VERY GRAVE...
I DON'T KNOW HOW MUCH LONGER SHE CAN HOLD THIS KINGDOM TOGETHER.
THE EXPLOSION MUST HAVE BROKEN THE OUTER SHELL...
YOU'RE RIGHT. BAALIKAR STILL HAS TO TRAVEL THROUGH THE CATACOMBS TO FIND THE QUEEN.
WE HAVE TO PROTECT MY MOTHER OR ALL OF THIS IS FOR NAUGHT.
FINALLY, ARE WE GOING TO FIGHT SOMETHING?
NO, MORGAN...
WE'RE GOING TO FIGHT **EVERYTHING.**

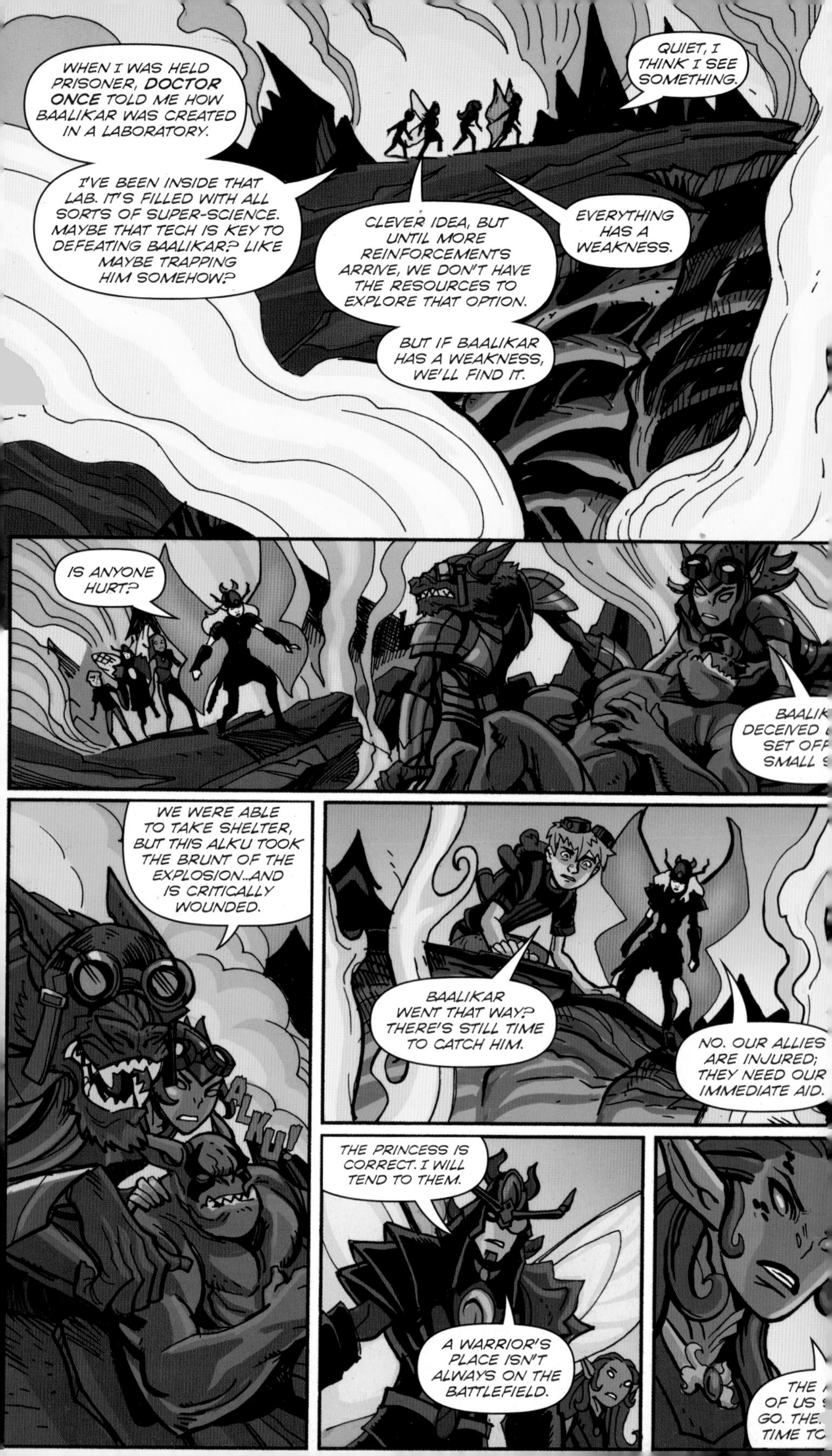
WHEN I WAS HELD PRISONER, DOCTOR ONCE TOLD ME HOW BAALIKAR WAS CREATED IN A LABORATORY.
I'VE BEEN INSIDE THAT LAB. IT'S FILLED WITH ALL SORTS OF SUPER-SCIENCE. MAYBE THAT TECH IS KEY TO DEFEATING BAALIKAR? LIKE MAYBE TRAPPING HIM SOMEHOW?
CLEVER IDEA, BUT UNTIL MORE REINFORCEMENTS ARRIVE, WE DON'T HAVE THE RESOURCES TO EXPLORE THAT OPTION.
BUT IF BAALIKAR HAS A WEAKNESS, WE'LL FIND IT.
EVERYTHING HAS A WEAKNESS.
QUIET, I THINK I SEE SOMETHING.
IS ANYONE HURT?
WE WERE ABLE TO TAKE SHELTER, BUT THIS ALKU TOOK THE BRUNT OF THE EXPLOSION...AND IS CRITICALLY WOUNDED.
ALKU!
BAALIKAR WENT THAT WAY? THERE'S STILL TIME TO CATCH HIM.
NO. OUR ALLIES ARE INJURED; THEY NEED OUR IMMEDIATE AID.
THE PRINCESS IS CORRECT. I WILL TEND TO THEM.
A WARRIOR'S PLACE ISN'T ALWAYS ON THE BATTLEFIELD.

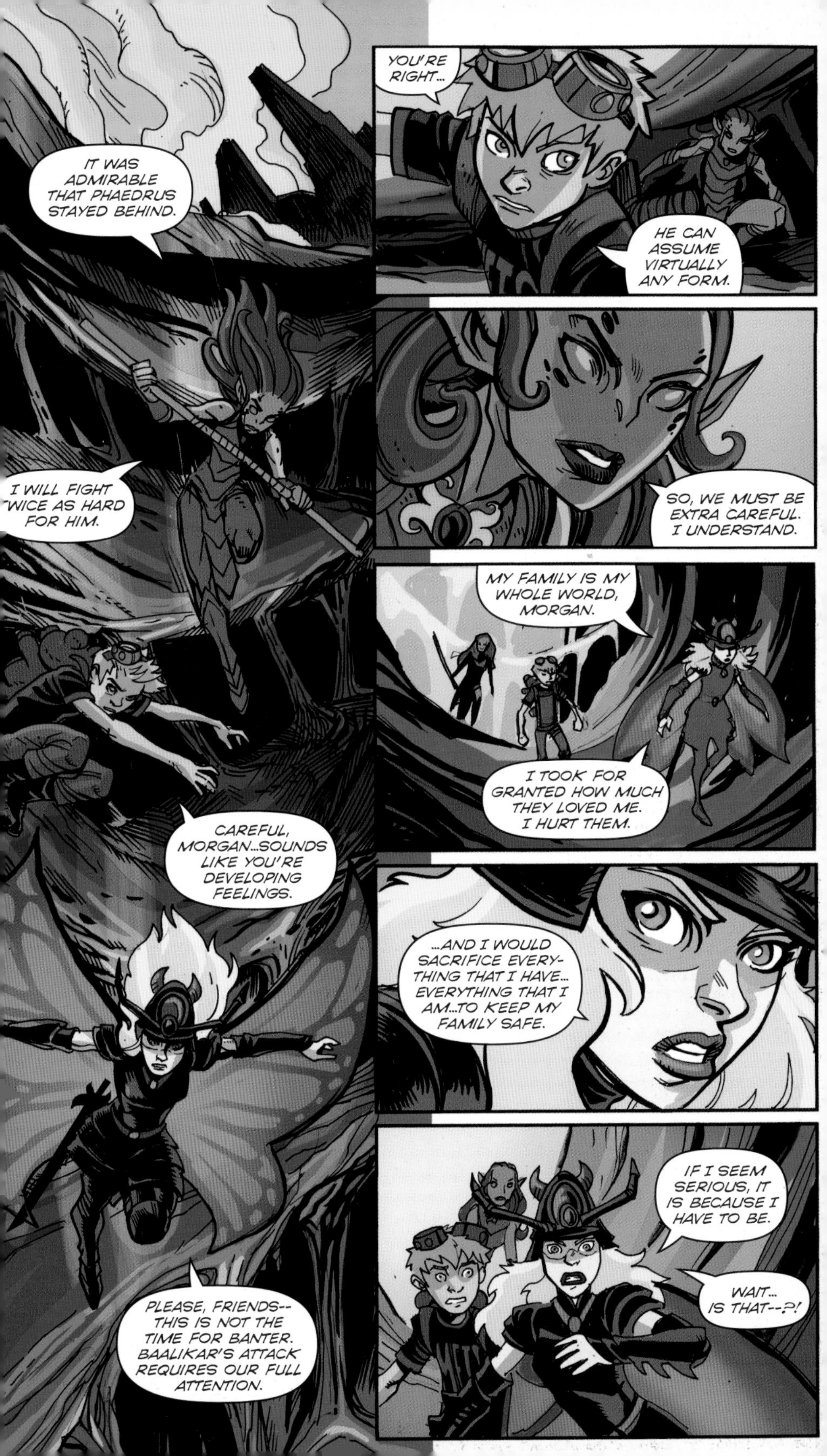

IT WAS ADMIRABLE THAT PHAEDRUS STAYED BEHIND.
I WILL FIGHT TWICE AS HARD FOR HIM.
CAREFUL, MORGAN...SOUNDS LIKE YOU'RE DEVELOPING FEELINGS.
PLEASE, FRIENDS-- THIS IS NOT THE TIME FOR BANTER. BAALIKAR'S ATTACK REQUIRES OUR FULL ATTENTION.
YOU'RE RIGHT...
HE CAN ASSUME VIRTUALLY ANY FORM.
SO, WE MUST BE EXTRA CAREFUL. I UNDERSTAND.
MY FAMILY IS MY WHOLE WORLD, MORGAN.
I TOOK FOR GRANTED HOW MUCH THEY LOVED ME. I HURT THEM.
...AND I WOULD SACRIFICE EVERY-THING THAT I HAVE... EVERYTHING THAT I AM...TO KEEP MY FAMILY SAFE.
IF I SEEM SERIOUS, IT IS BECAUSE I HAVE TO BE.
WAIT... IS THAT--?!

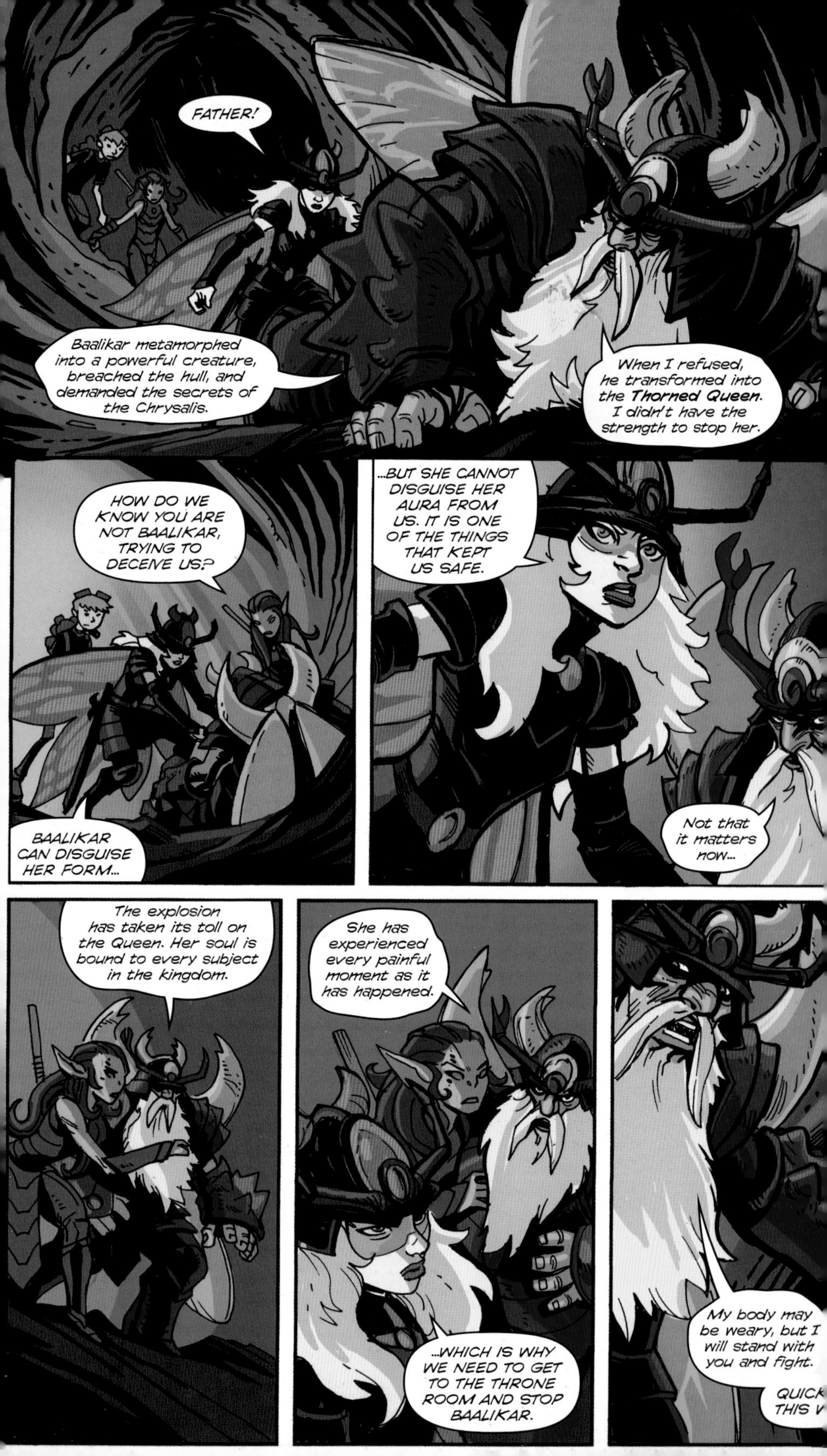
FATHER!
Baalikar metamorphed into a powerful creature, breached the hull, and demanded the secrets of the Chrysalis.
When I refused, he transformed into the **Thorned Queen**. I didn't have the strength to stop her.
HOW DO WE KNOW YOU ARE NOT BAALIKAR, TRYING TO DECEIVE US?
BAALIKAR CAN DISGUISE HER FORM...
...BUT SHE CANNOT DISGUISE HER AURA FROM US. IT IS ONE OF THE THINGS THAT KEPT US SAFE.
Not that it matters now...
The explosion has taken its toll on the Queen. Her soul is bound to every subject in the kingdom.
She has experienced every painful moment as it has happened.
...WHICH IS WHY WE NEED TO GET TO THE THRONE ROOM AND STOP BAALIKAR.
My body may be weary, but I will stand with you and fight.

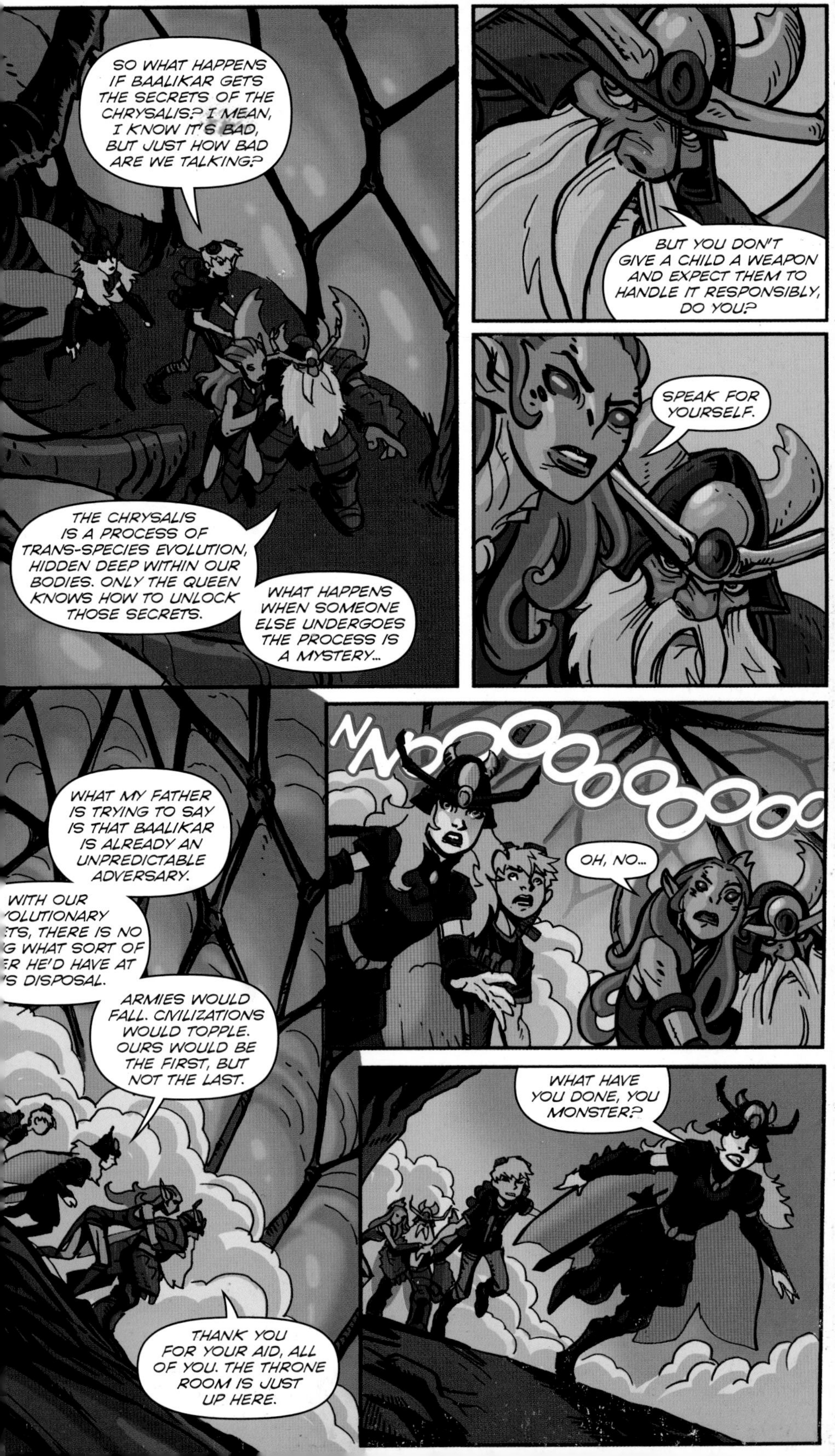
SO WHAT HAPPENS IF BAALIKAR GETS THE SECRETS OF THE CHRYSALIS? I MEAN, I KNOW IT'S BAD, BUT JUST HOW BAD ARE WE TALKING?
THE CHRYSALIS IS A PROCESS OF TRANS-SPECIES EVOLUTION, HIDDEN DEEP WITHIN OUR BODIES. ONLY THE QUEEN KNOWS HOW TO UNLOCK THOSE SECRETS.
WHAT HAPPENS WHEN SOMEONE ELSE UNDERGOES THE PROCESS IS A MYSTERY...
BUT YOU DON'T GIVE A CHILD A WEAPON AND EXPECT THEM TO HANDLE IT RESPONSIBLY, DO YOU?
SPEAK FOR YOURSELF.
WHAT MY FATHER IS TRYING TO SAY IS THAT BAALIKAR IS ALREADY AN UNPREDICTABLE ADVERSARY.
WITH OUR VOLUTIONARY ETS, THERE IS NO G WHAT SORT OF ER HE'D HAVE AT 'S DISPOSAL.
ARMIES WOULD FALL. CIVILIZATIONS WOULD TOPPLE. OURS WOULD BE THE FIRST, BUT NOT THE LAST.
THANK YOU FOR YOUR AID, ALL OF YOU. THE THRONE ROOM IS JUST UP HERE.
NNOOOOOOOOOOOO
OH, NO...
WHAT HAVE YOU DONE, YOU MONSTER?

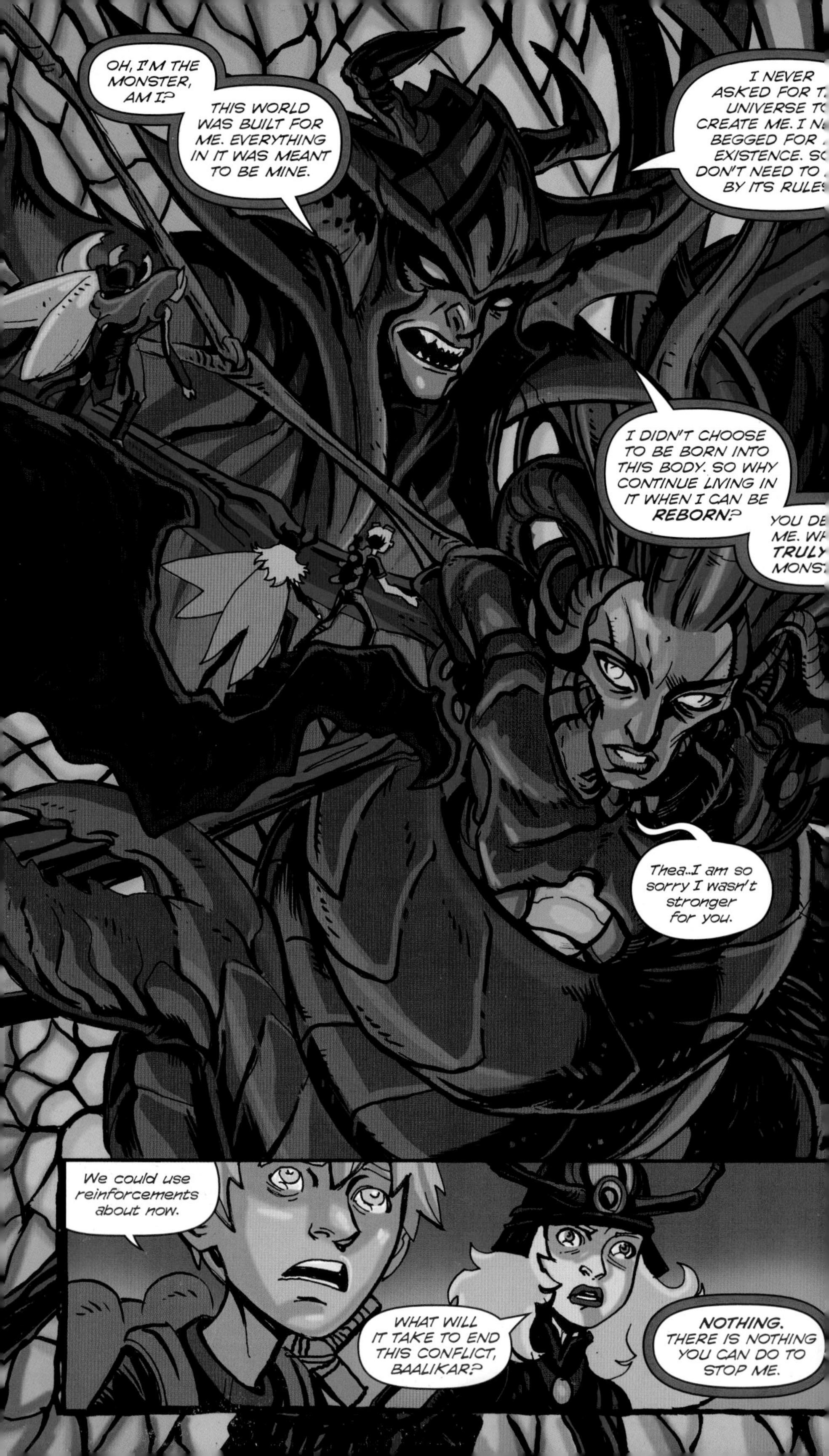
OH, I'M THE MONSTER, AM I?
THIS WORLD WAS BUILT FOR ME. EVERYTHING IN IT WAS MEANT TO BE MINE.
I NEVER ASKED FOR UNIVERSE CREATE ME. BEGGED FOR EXISTENCE. DON'T NEED TO BY ITS
I DIDN'T CHOOSE TO BE BORN INTO THIS BODY. SO WHY CONTINUE LIVING IN IT WHEN I CAN BE REBORN?
YOU ME. TRULY
Thea..I am so sorry I wasn't stronger for you.
We could use reinforcements about now.
WHAT WILL IT TAKE TO END THIS CONFLICT, BAALIKAR?
NOTHING. THERE IS NOTHING YOU CAN DO TO STOP ME.

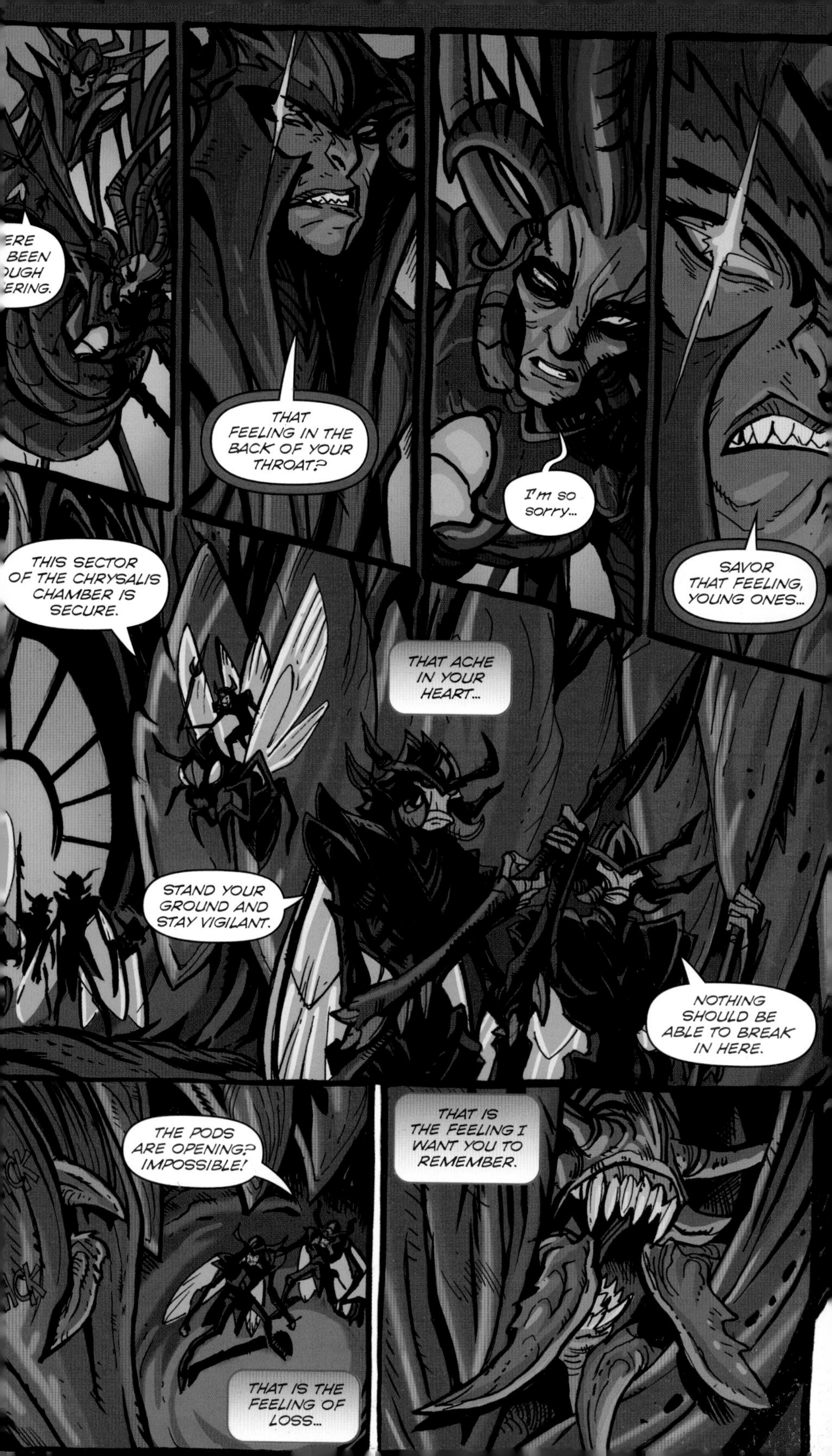
ERE BEEN OUGH ERING.
THAT FEELING IN THE BACK OF YOUR THROAT?
I'm so sorry...
SAVOR THAT FEELING, YOUNG ONES...
THIS SECTOR OF THE CHRYSALIS CHAMBER IS SECURE.
THAT ACHE IN YOUR HEART...
STAND YOUR GROUND AND STAY VIGILANT.
NOTHING SHOULD BE ABLE TO BREAK IN HERE.
THE PODS ARE OPENING? IMPOSSIBLE!
THAT IS THE FEELING OF LOSS...
THAT IS THE FEELING I WANT YOU TO REMEMBER.

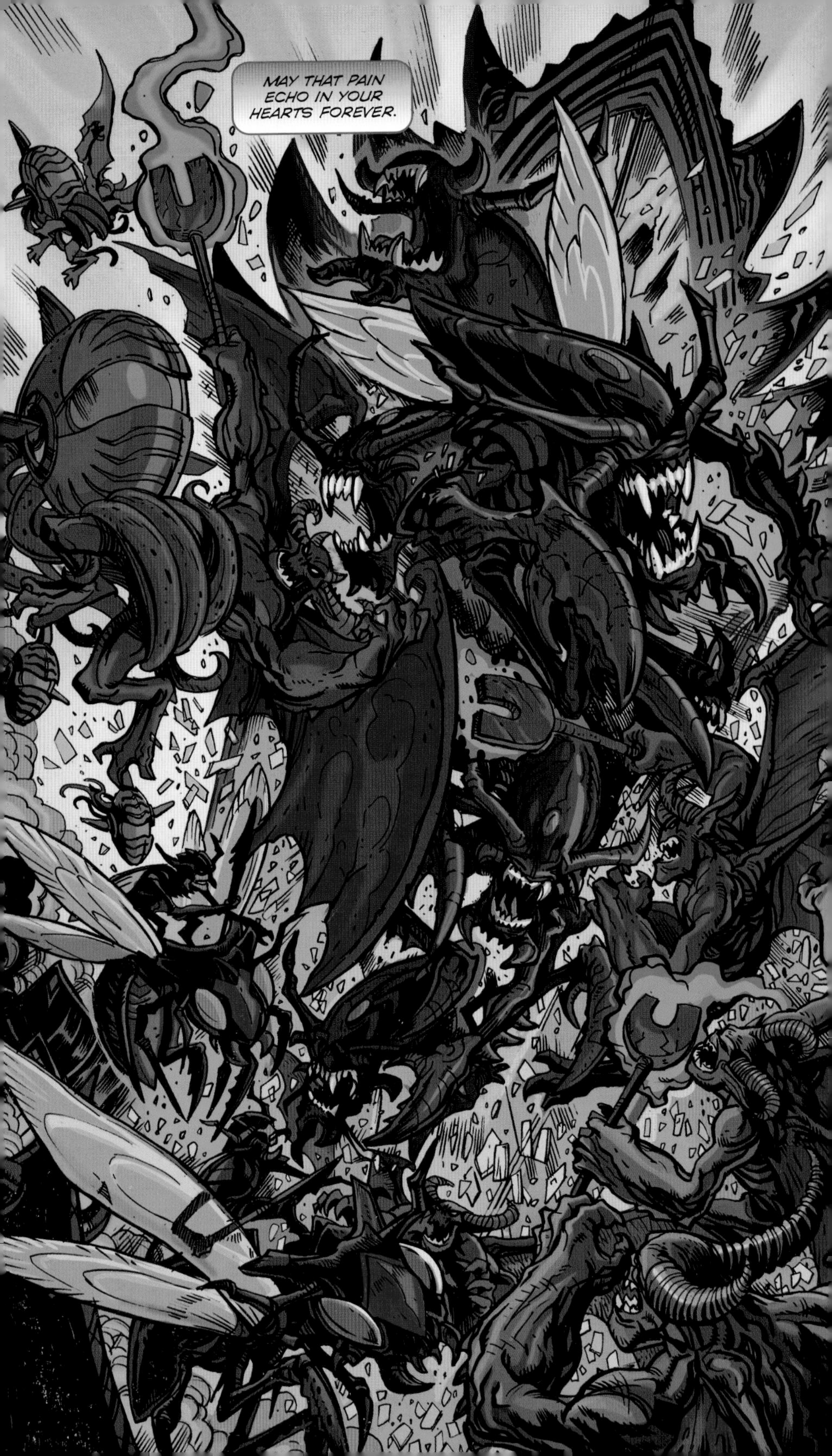
MAY THAT PAIN ECHO IN YOUR HEARTS FOREVER.

CHAPTER TEN

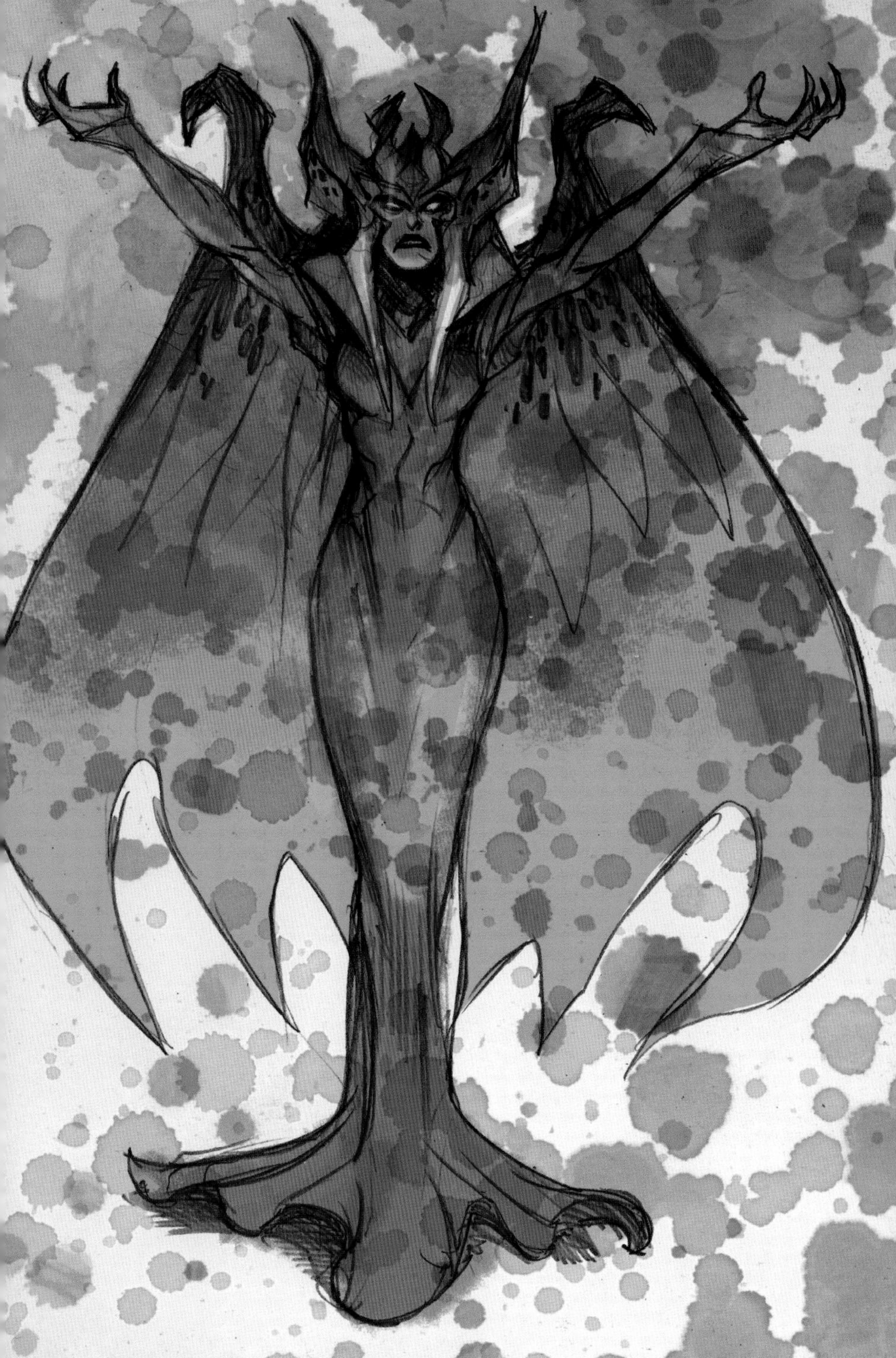

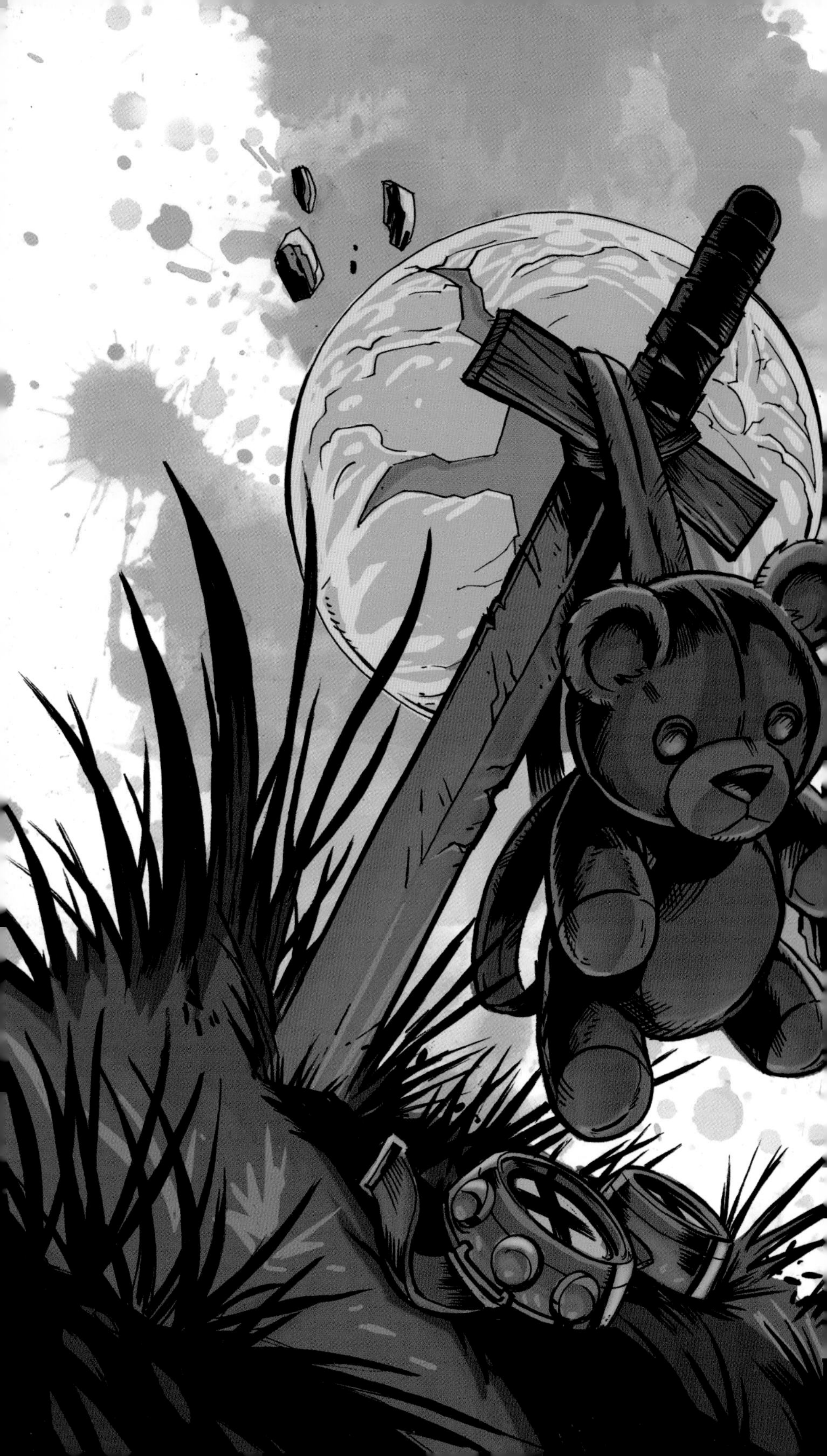

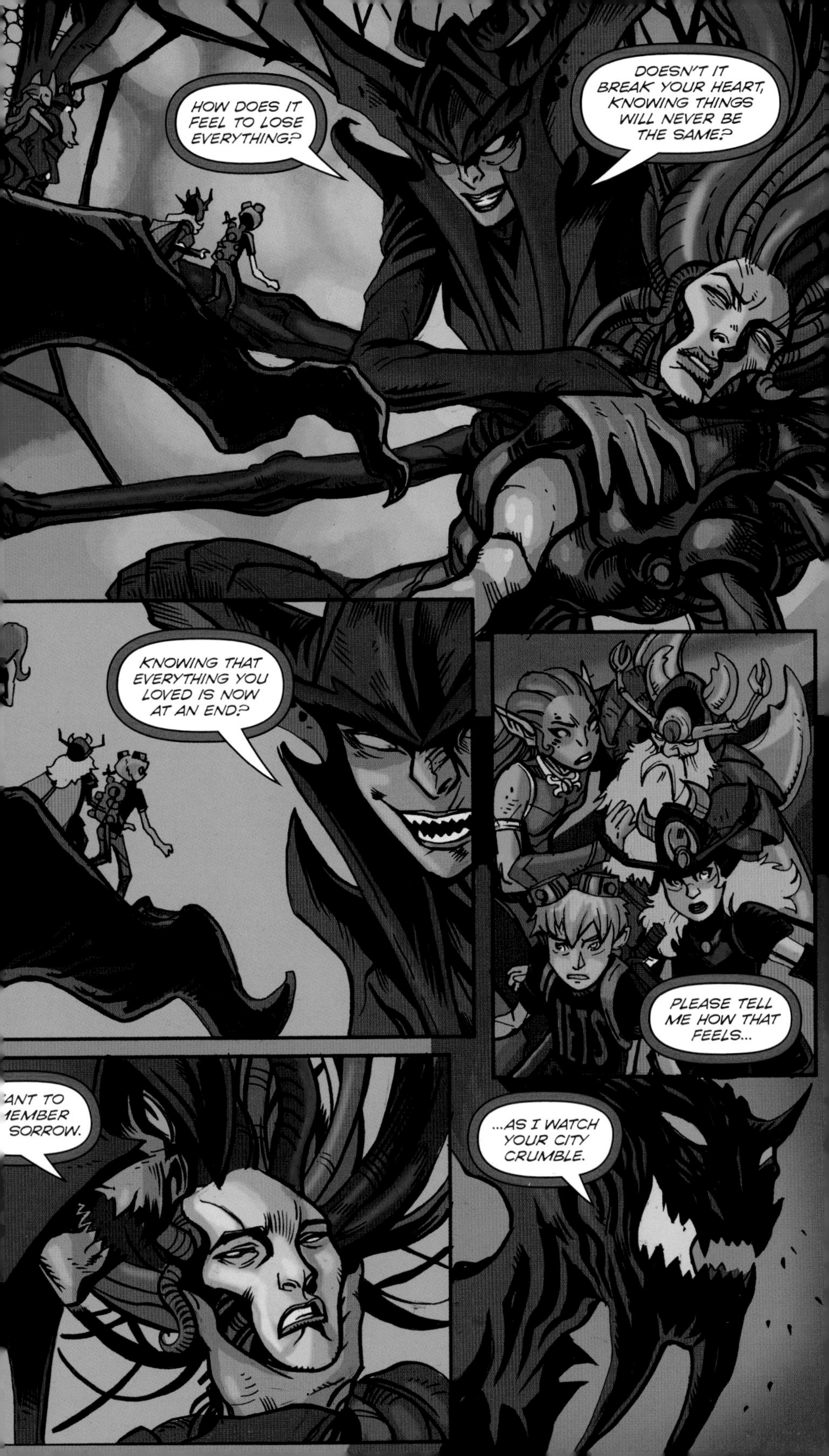
HOW DOES IT FEEL TO LOSE EVERYTHING?
DOESN'T IT BREAK YOUR HEART, KNOWING THINGS WILL NEVER BE THE SAME?
KNOWING THAT EVERYTHING YOU LOVED IS NOW AT AN END?
PLEASE TELL ME HOW THAT FEELS...
ANT TO MEMBER SORROW.
...AS I WATCH YOUR CITY CRUMBLE.

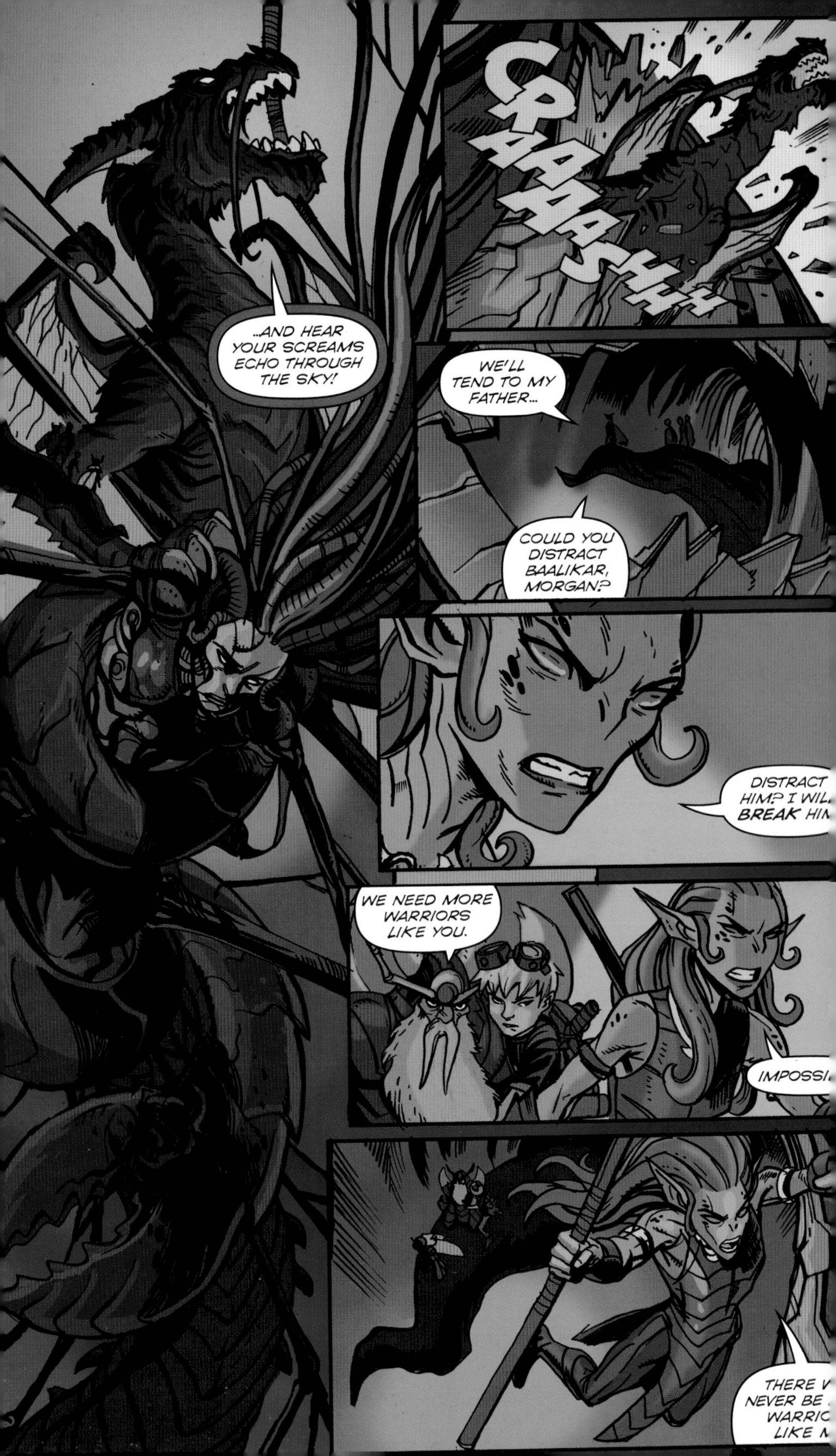

CRAAAASHHH
...AND HEAR YOUR SCREAMS ECHO THROUGH THE SKY!
WE'LL TEND TO MY FATHER...
COULD YOU DISTRACT BAALIKAR, MORGAN?
DISTRACT HIM? I WIL
BREAK HIM
WE NEED MORE WARRIORS LIKE YOU.
IMPOSSI
THERE W
NEVER BE
WARRIO
LIKE M

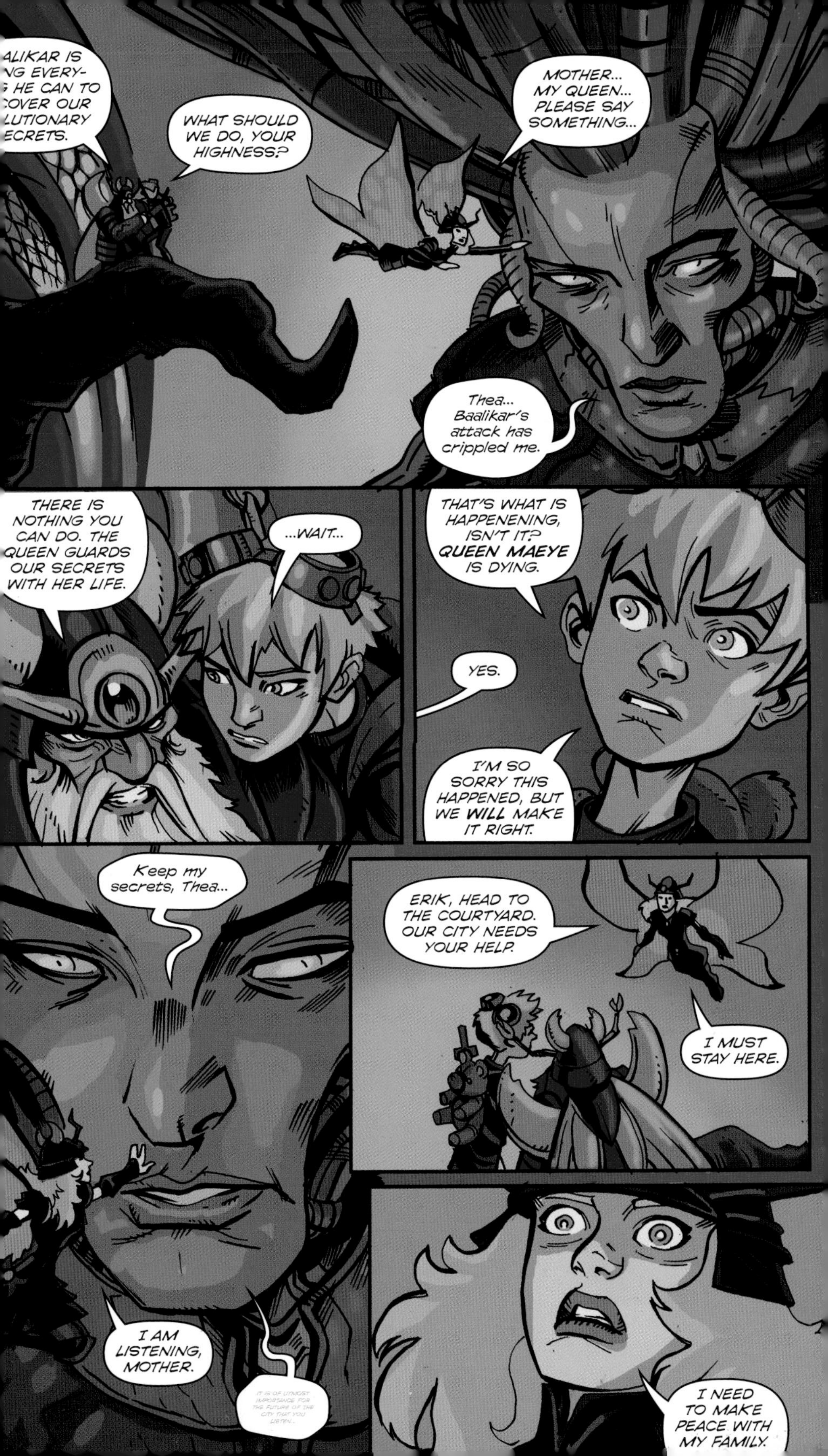
ALIKAR IS NG EVERY- G HE CAN TO COVER OUR LUTIONARY ECRETS.
WHAT SHOULD WE DO, YOUR HIGHNESS?
MOTHER... MY QUEEN... PLEASE SAY SOMETHING...
Thea... Baalikar's attack has crippled me.
THERE IS NOTHING YOU CAN DO. THE QUEEN GUARDS OUR SECRETS WITH HER LIFE.
...WAIT...
THAT'S WHAT IS HAPPENENING, ISN'T IT? QUEEN MAEYE IS DYING.
YES.
I'M SO SORRY THIS HAPPENED, BUT WE WILL MAKE IT RIGHT.
Keep my secrets, Thea...
I AM LISTENING, MOTHER.
IT IS OF UTMOST IMPORTANCE FOR THE FUTURE OF THE CITY THAT YOU LISTEN...
ERIK, HEAD TO THE COURTYARD. OUR CITY NEEDS YOUR HELP.
I MUST STAY HERE.
I NEED TO MAKE PEACE WITH MY FAMILY.

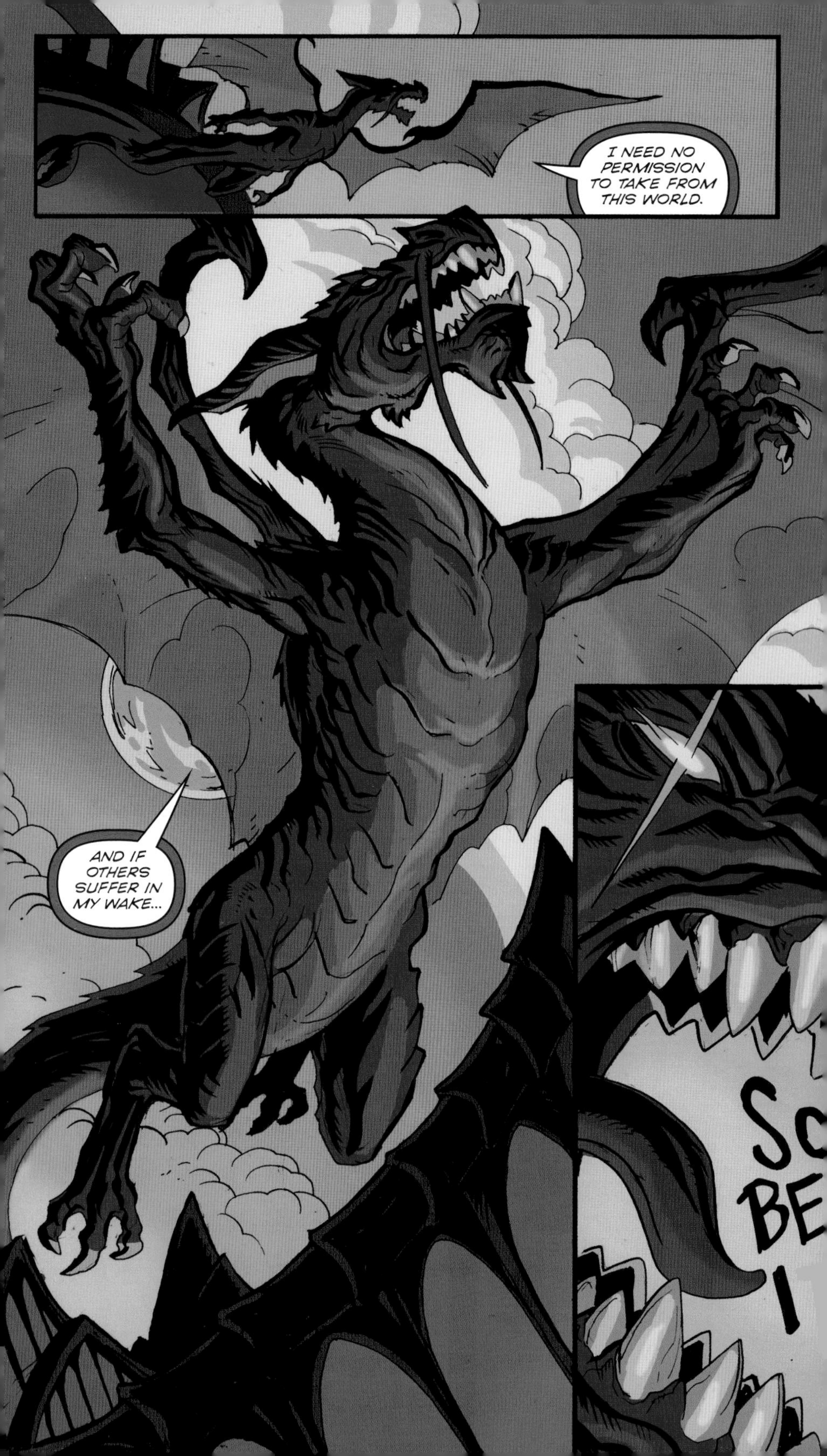
I NEED NO PERMISSION TO TAKE FROM THIS WORLD.
AND IF OTHERS SUFFER IN MY WAKE...

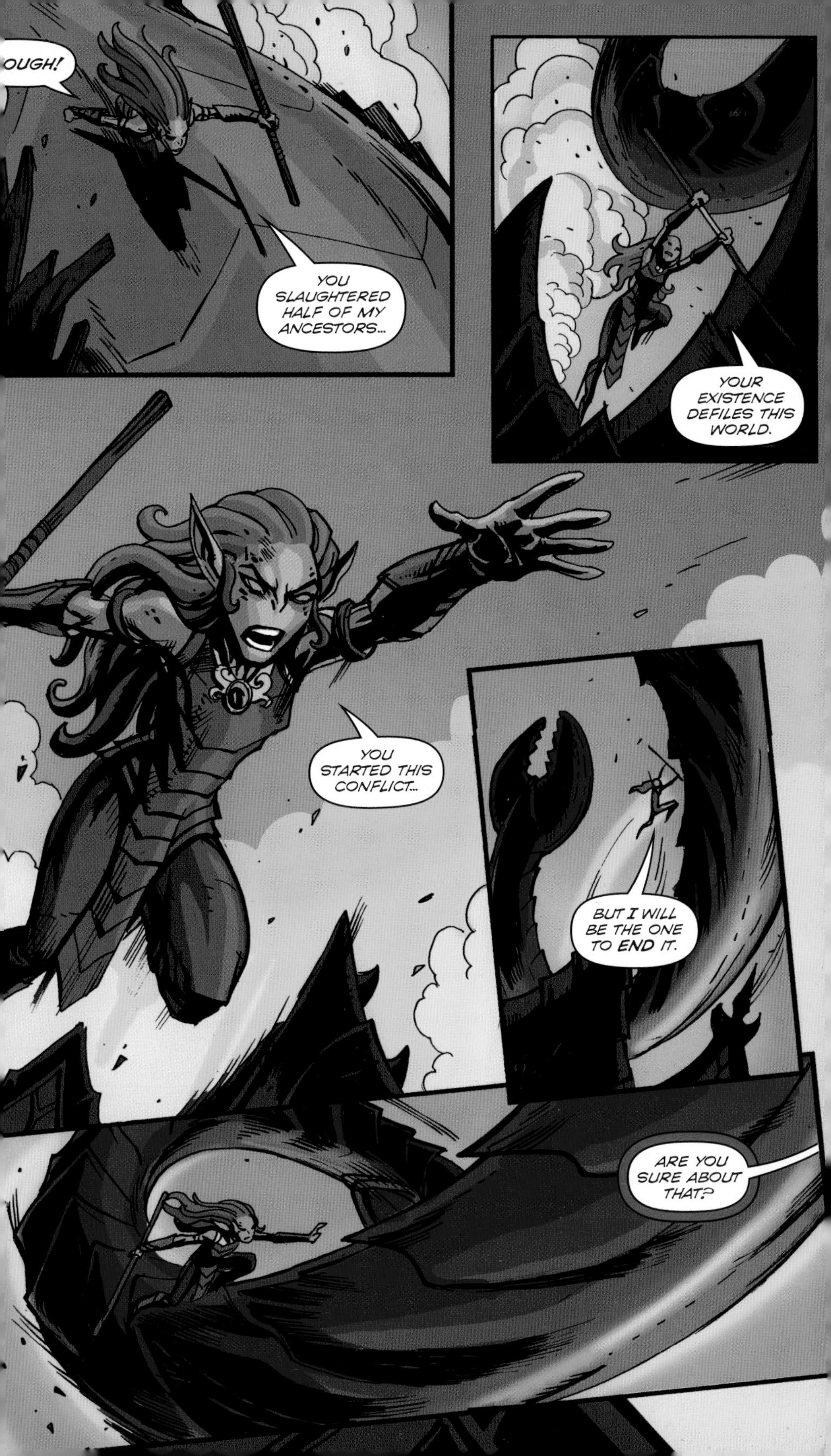
OUGH!
YOU SLAUGHTERED HALF OF MY ANCESTORS...
YOUR EXISTENCE DEFILES THIS WORLD.
YOU STARTED THIS CONFLICT...
BUT I WILL BE THE ONE TO END IT.
ARE YOU SURE ABOUT THAT?

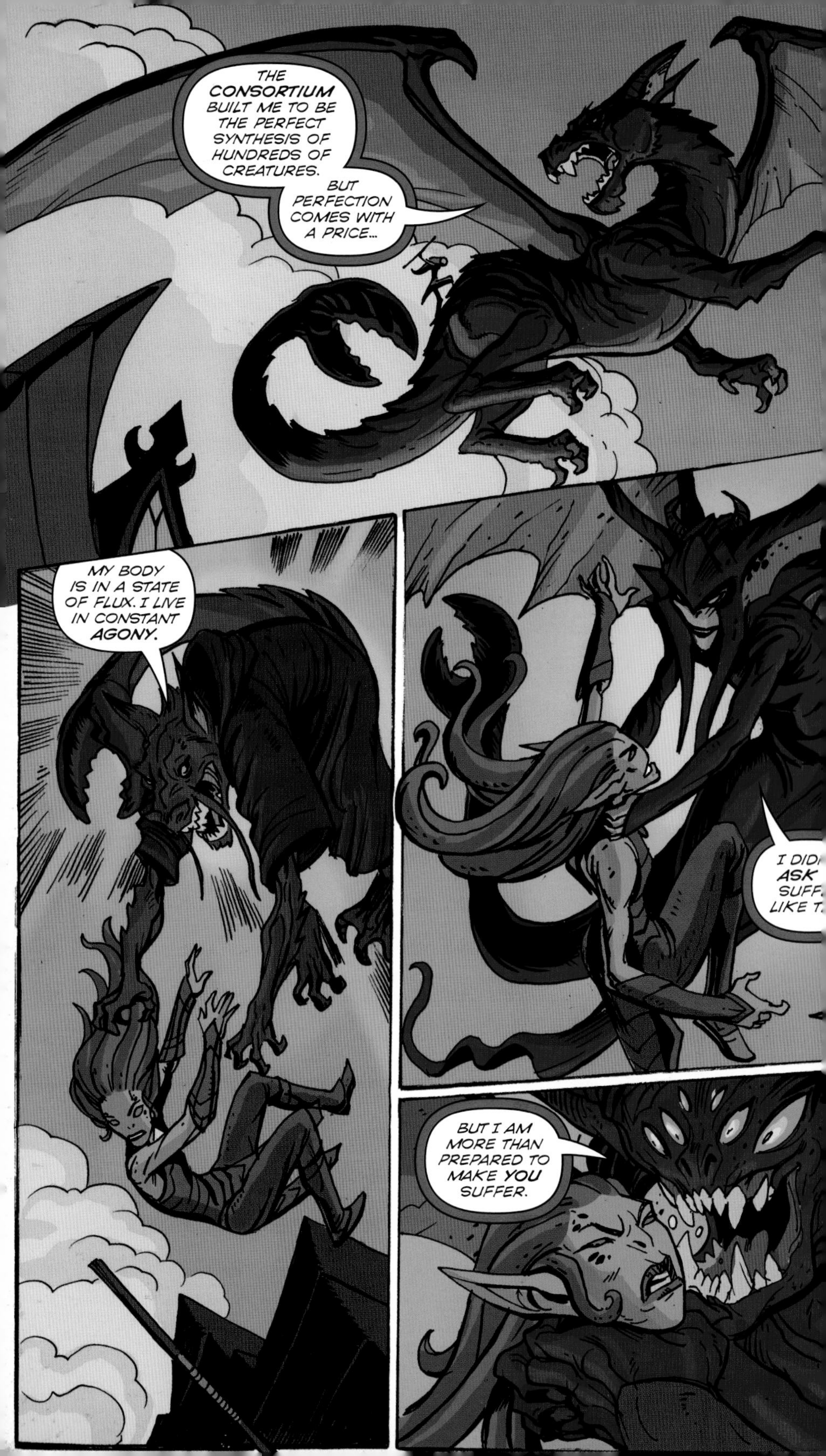

THE CONSORTIUM BUILT ME TO BE THE PERFECT SYNTHESIS OF HUNDREDS OF CREATURES.
BUT PERFECTION COMES WITH A PRICE...
MY BODY IS IN A STATE OF FLUX. I LIVE IN CONSTANT AGONY.
I DID ASK SUFF LIKE T
BUT I AM MORE THAN PREPARED TO MAKE YOU SUFFER.

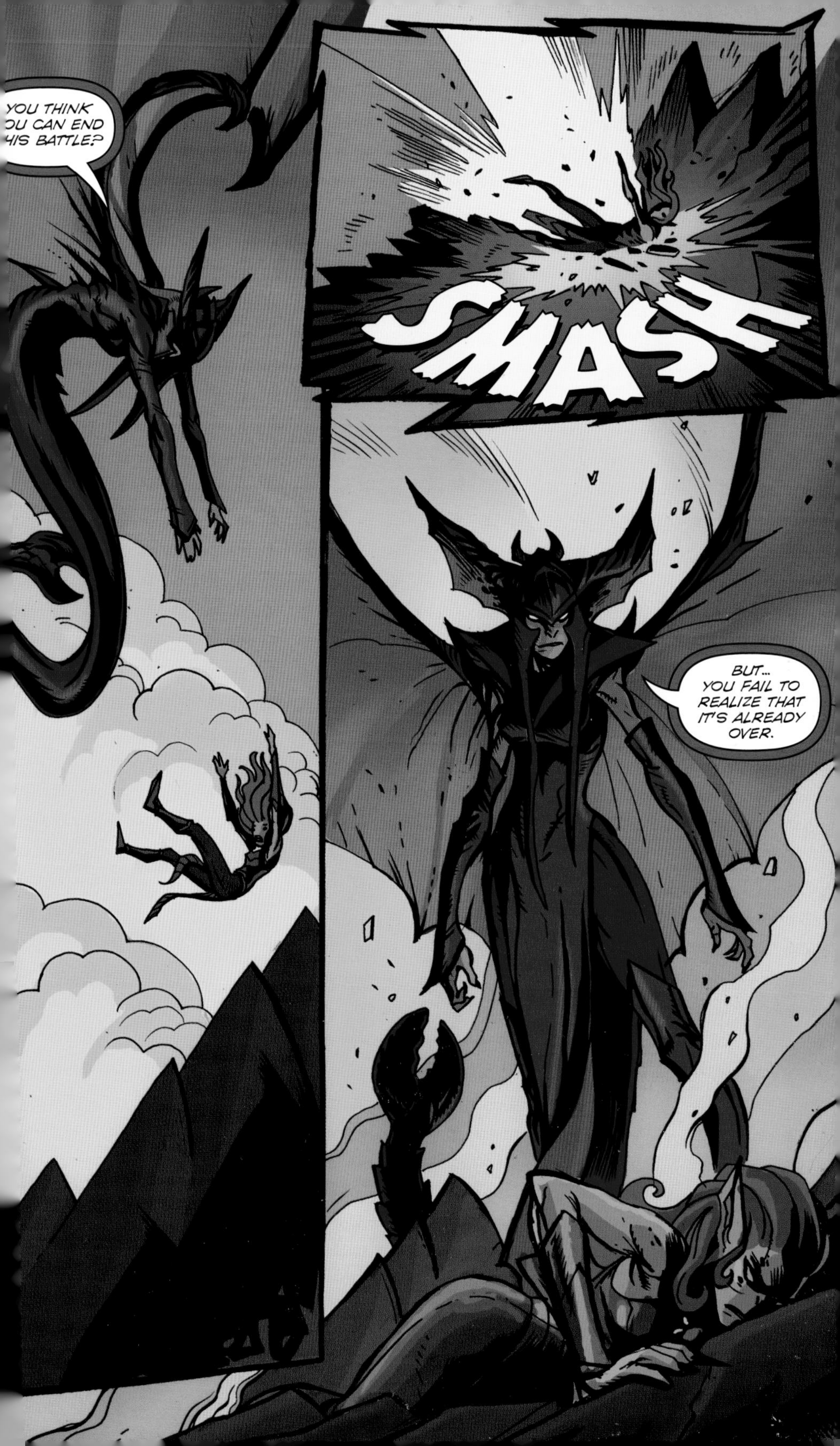
YOU THINK OU CAN END HIS BATTLE?
SMASH
BUT... YOU FAIL TO REALIZE THAT IT'S ALREADY OVER.

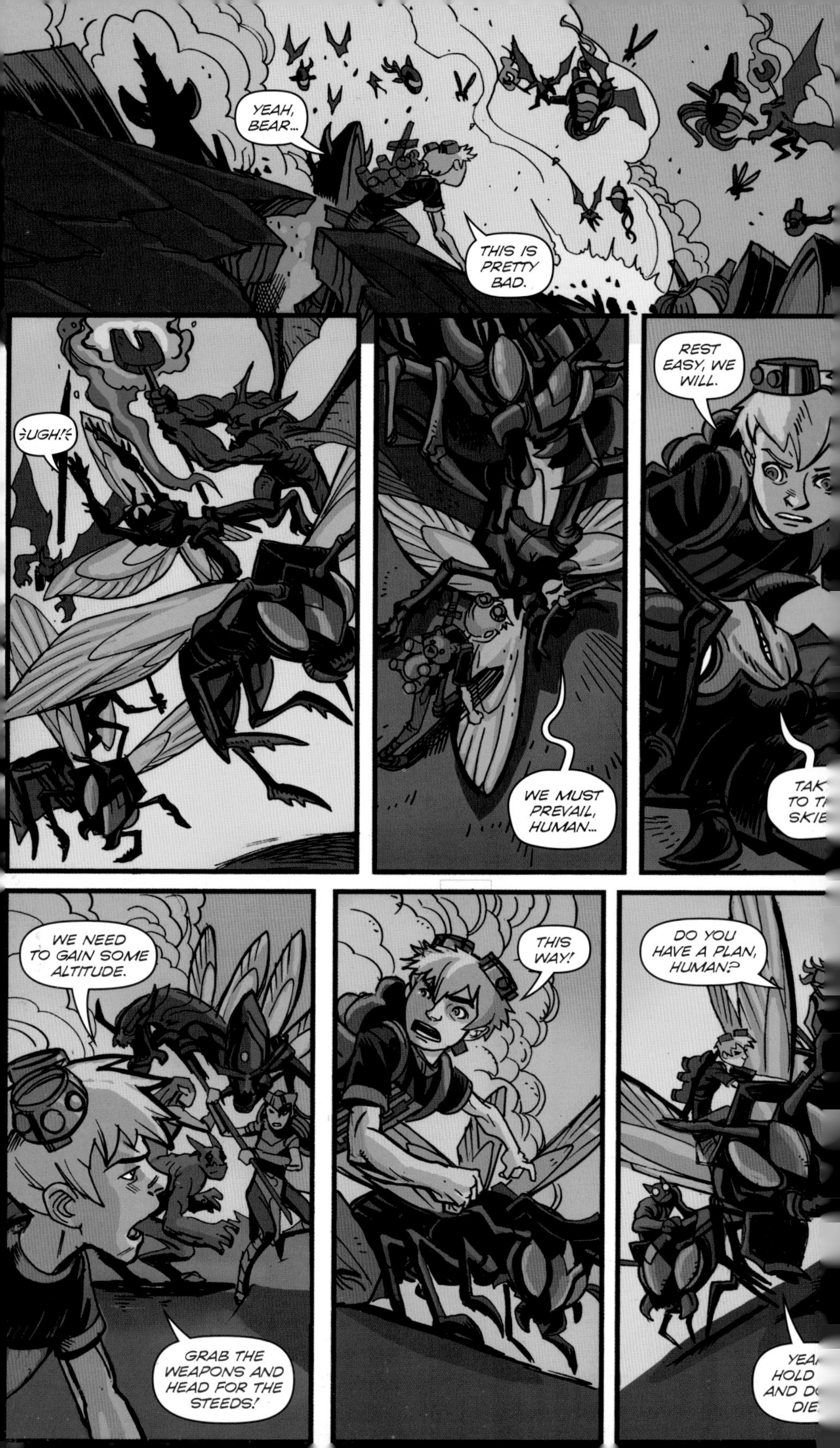
YEAH, BEAR...
THIS IS PRETTY BAD.
UGH!
WE MUST PREVAIL, HUMAN...
REST EASY, WE WILL.
WE NEED TO GAIN SOME ALTITUDE.
GRAB THE WEAPONS AND HEAD FOR THE STEEDS!
THIS WAY!
DO YOU HAVE A PLAN, HUMAN?

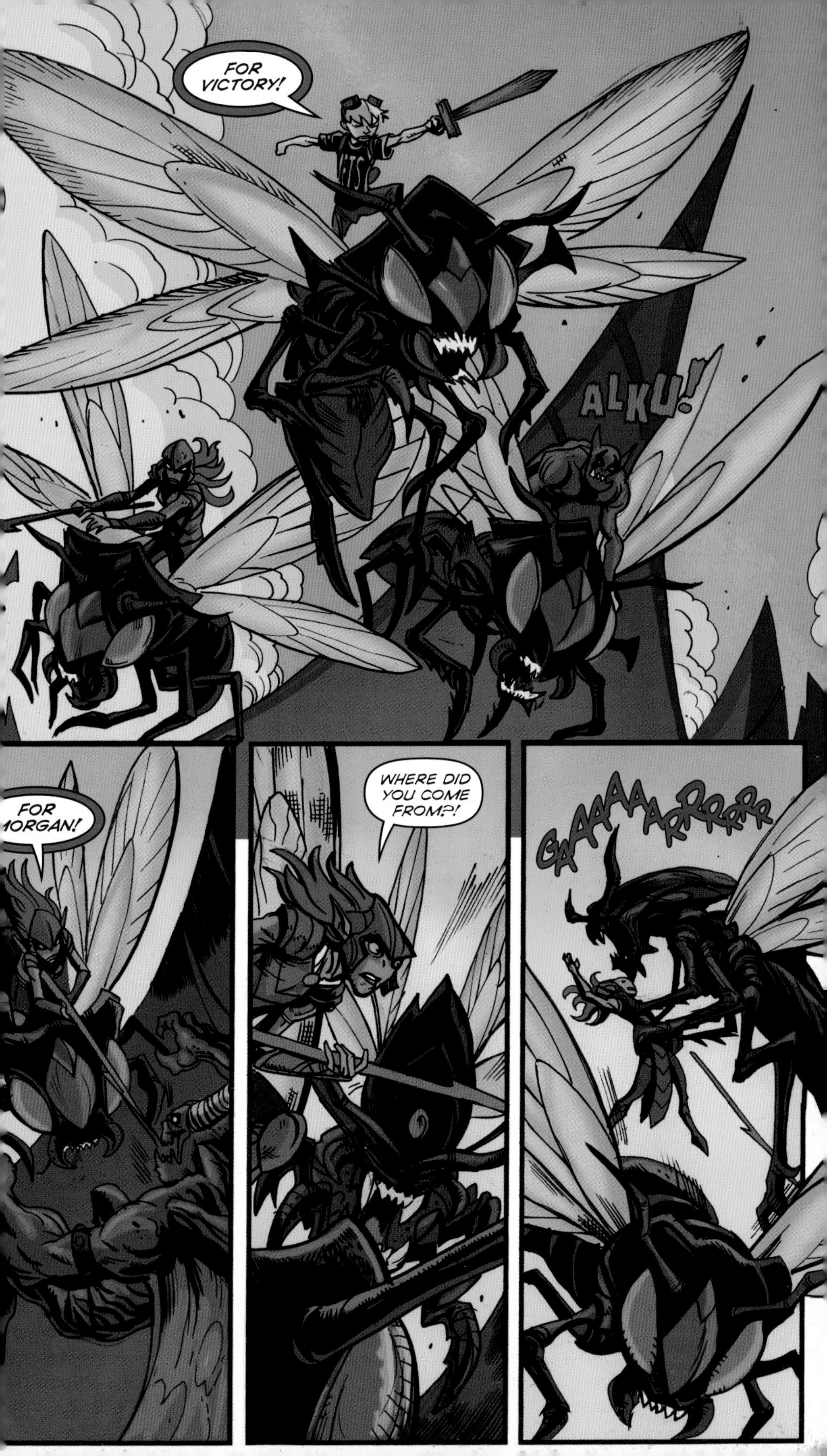
FOR VICTORY!
ALKU!
FOR MORGAN!
WHERE DID YOU COME FROM?!
GAAAAARRRRRR

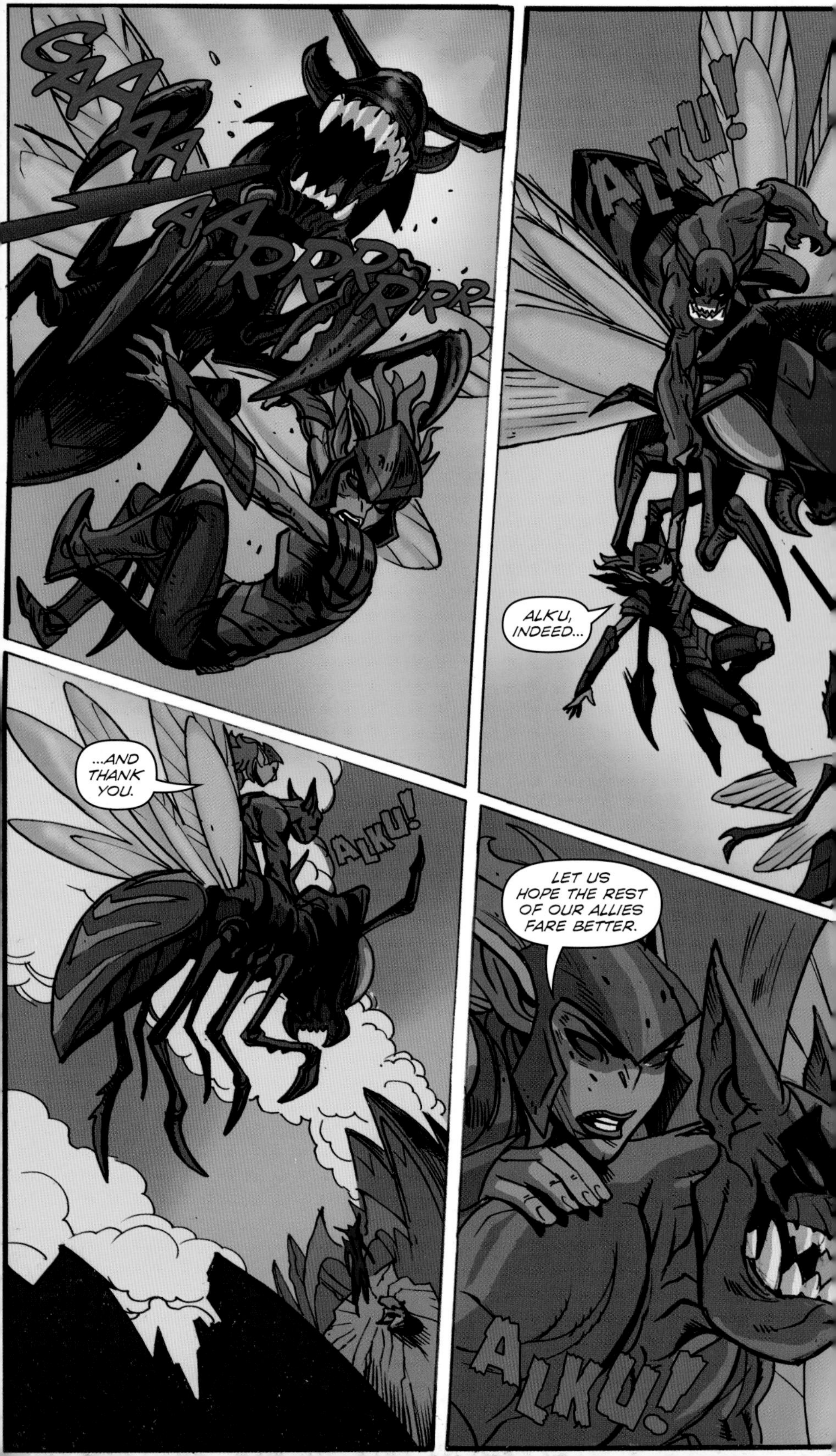
GAAAAA
AAARRRRRRRR
ALKU!
ALKU, INDEED...
...AND THANK YOU.
ALKU!
LET US HOPE THE REST OF OUR ALLIES FARE BETTER.
ALKU!

YOU'RE GETTING WEAKER...

HARDLY.

...WHAT ...NTED, ...IT, ...NG?

...CONFRONT ...BE WORTHY ...F YOUR ...LENTS?

I'LL LET YOU KNOW WHEN I FIND ONE.

{uff}

YES, PLEASE DO.

{uff}

I CAN COMPETE AT YOUR LEVEL.

...BUT YOU'LL NEVER COMPETE AT MINE.

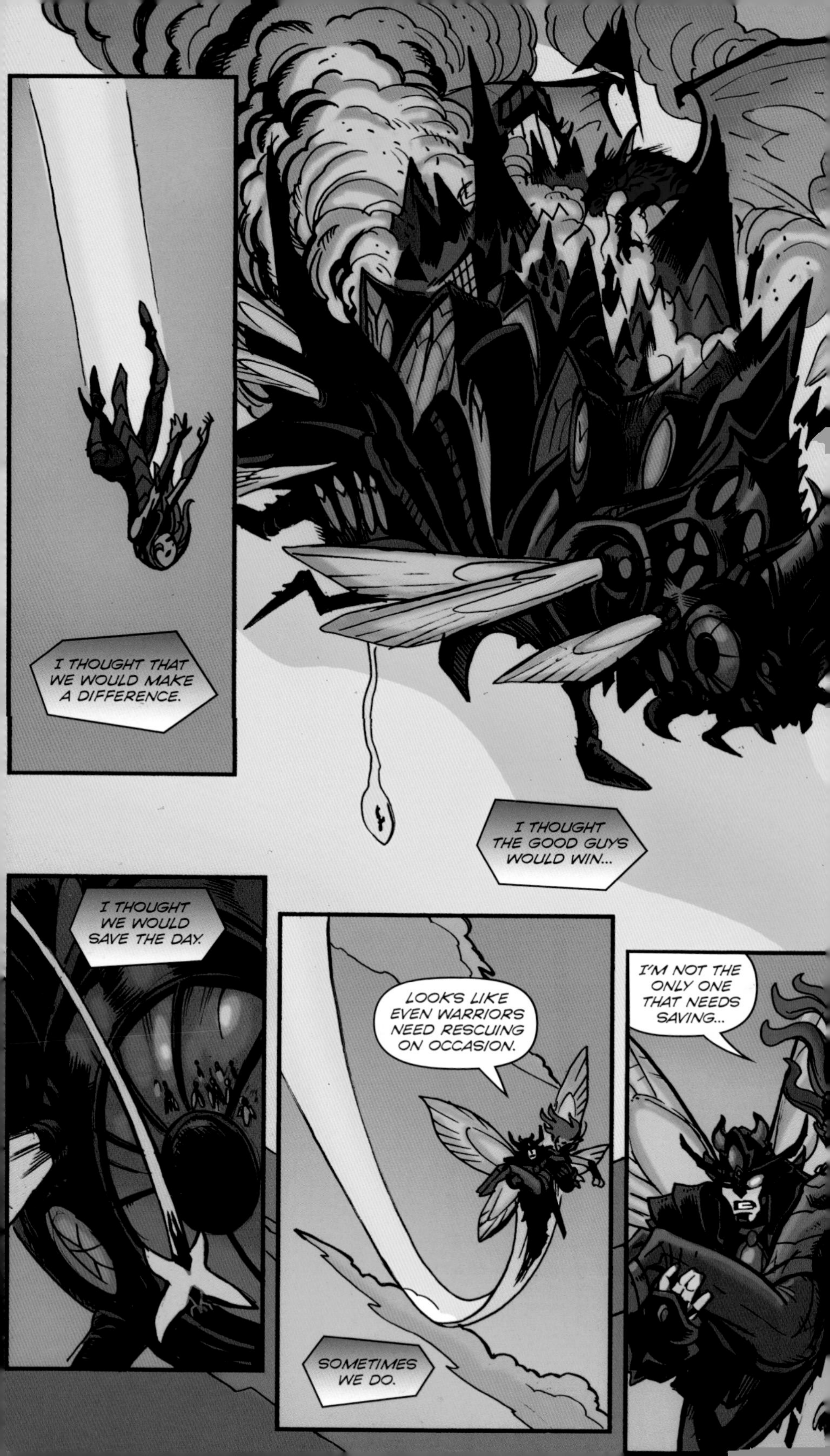

I THOUGHT THAT WE WOULD MAKE A DIFFERENCE.
I THOUGHT THE GOOD GUYS WOULD WIN...
I THOUGHT WE WOULD SAVE THE DAY.
LOOKS LIKE EVEN WARRIORS NEED RESCUING ON OCCASION.
SOMETIMES WE DO.
I'M NOT THE ONLY ONE THAT NEEDS SAVING...

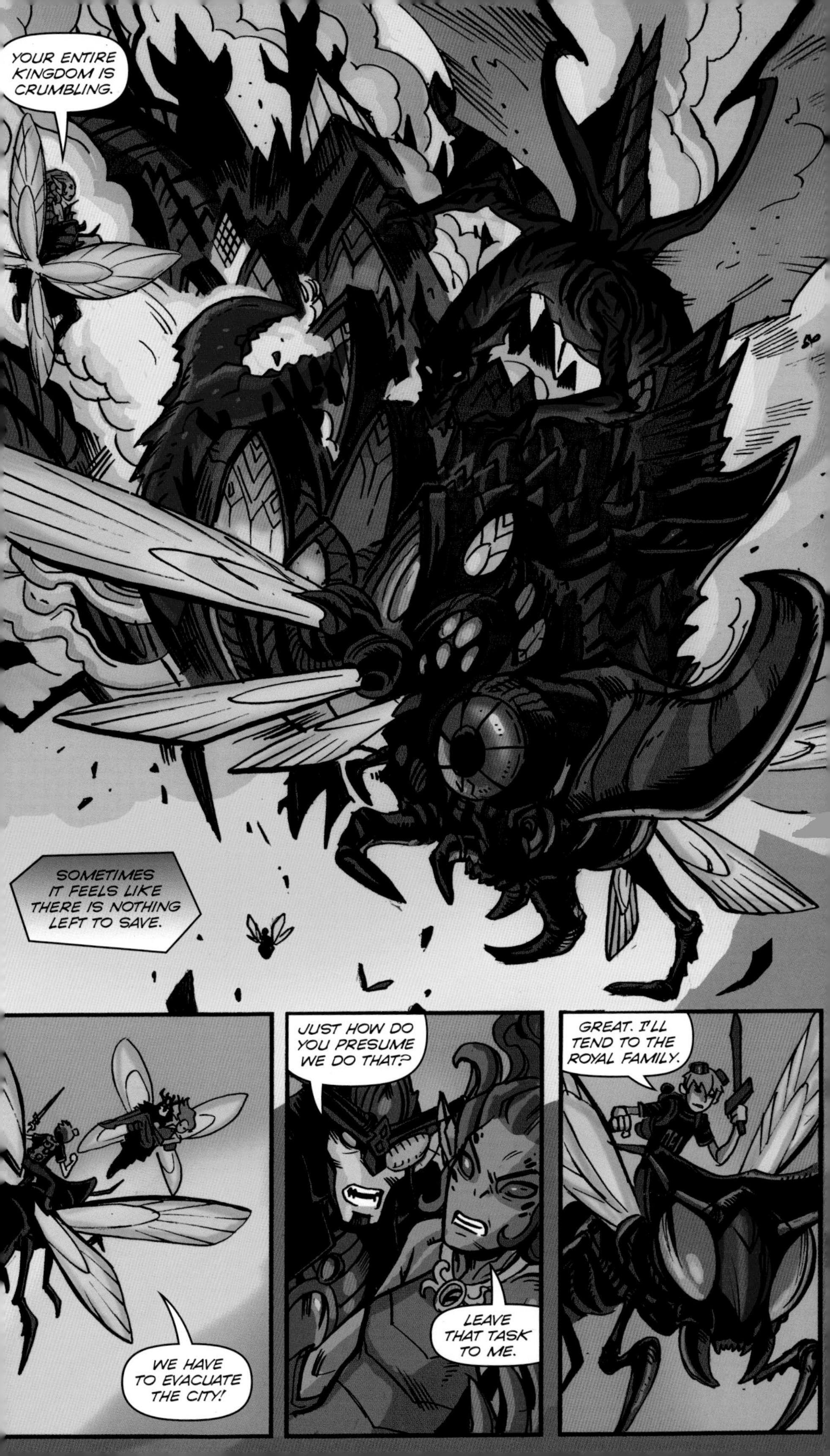
YOUR ENTIRE KINGDOM IS CRUMBLING.
SOMETIMES IT FEELS LIKE THERE IS NOTHING LEFT TO SAVE.
WE HAVE TO EVACUATE THE CITY!
JUST HOW DO YOU PRESUME WE DO THAT?
LEAVE THAT TASK TO ME.
GREAT. I'LL TEND TO THE ROYAL FAMILY.

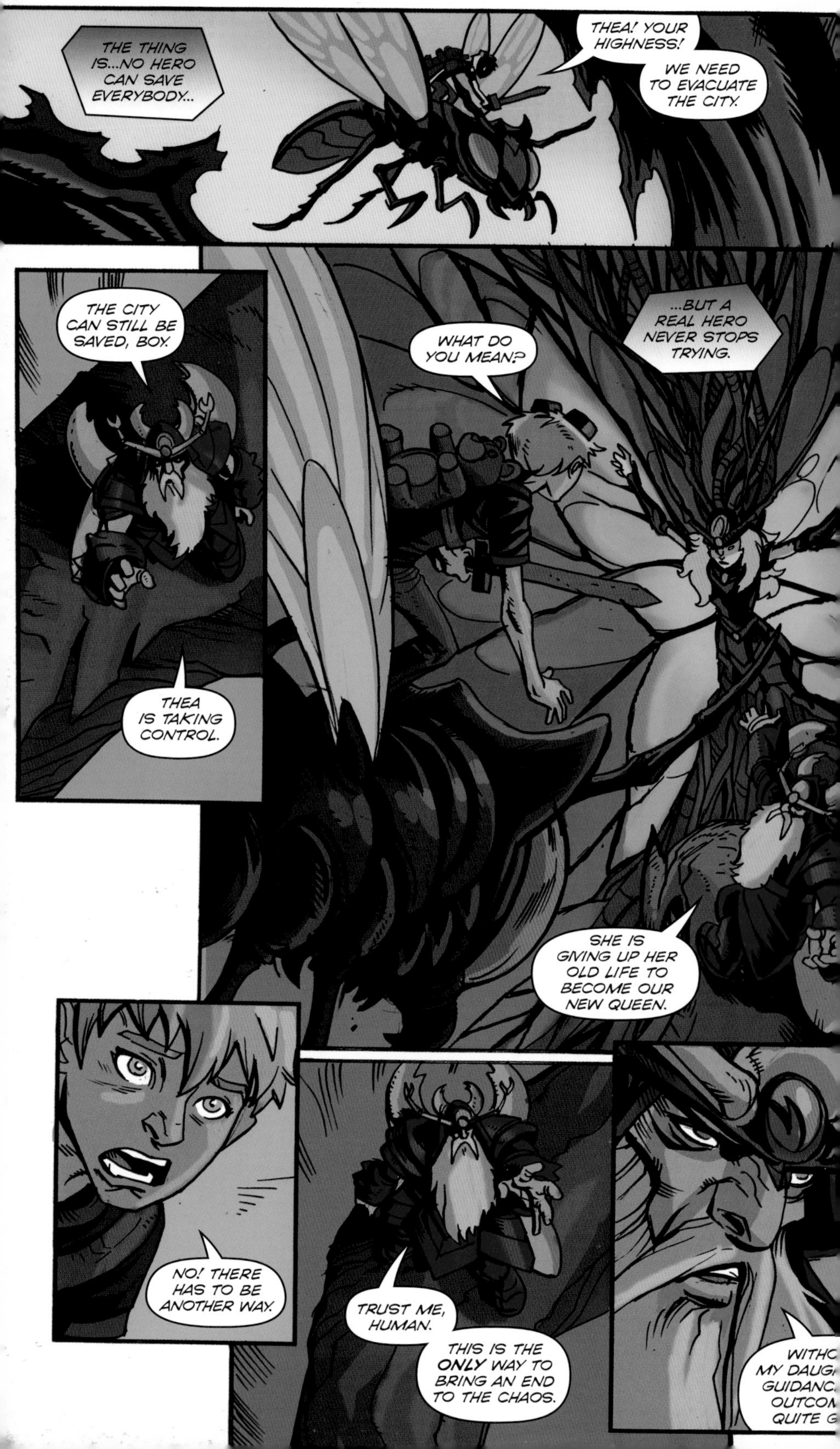
THE THING IS...NO HERO CAN SAVE EVERYBODY...
THEA! YOUR HIGHNESS!
WE NEED TO EVACUATE THE CITY.
THE CITY CAN STILL BE SAVED, BOY.
WHAT DO YOU MEAN?
...BUT A REAL HERO NEVER STOPS TRYING.
THEA IS TAKING CONTROL.
SHE IS GIVING UP HER OLD LIFE TO BECOME OUR NEW QUEEN.
NO! THERE HAS TO BE ANOTHER WAY.
TRUST ME, HUMAN.
THIS IS THE ONLY WAY TO BRING AN END TO THE CHAOS.

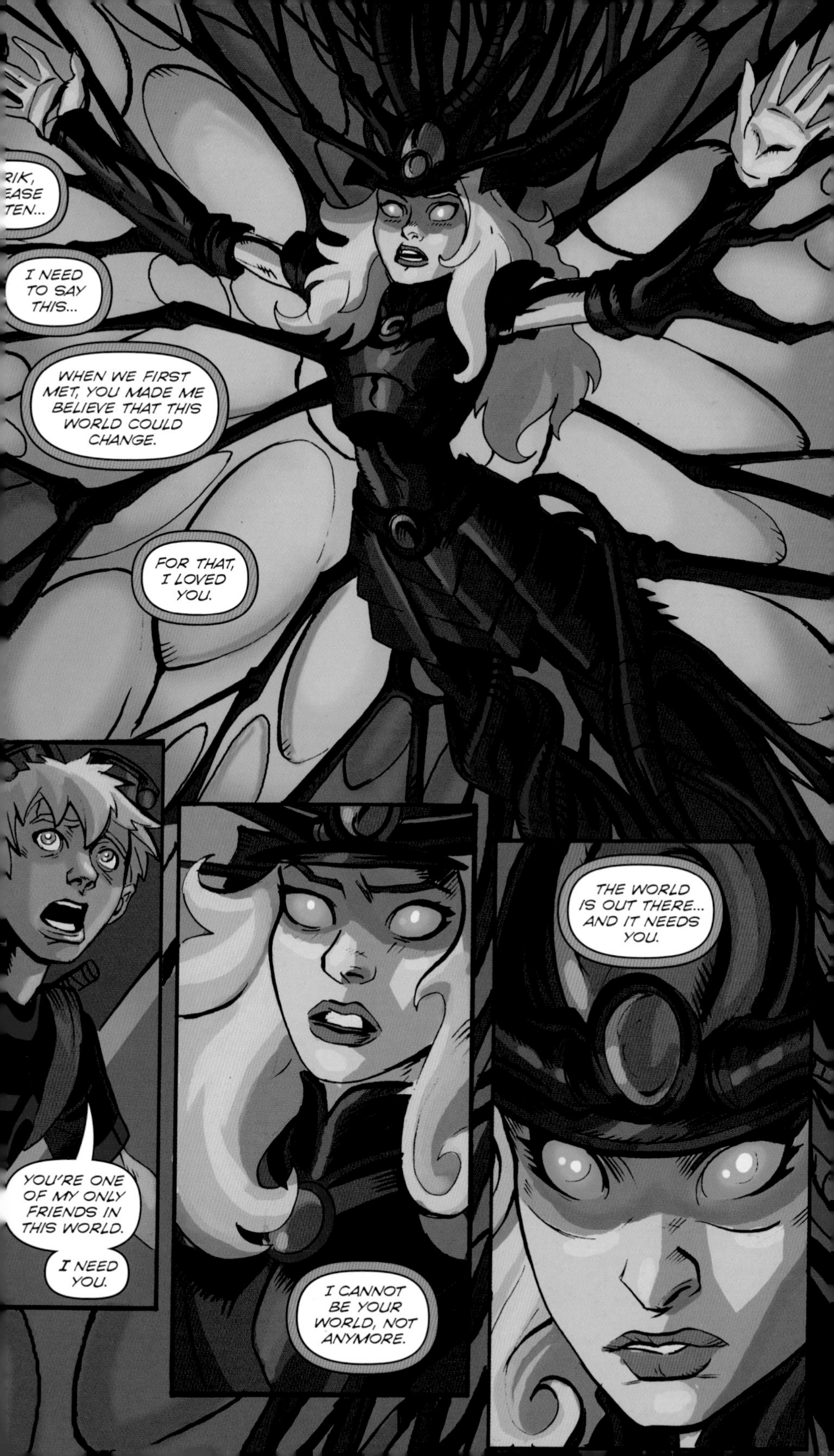
RIK, EASE TEN...
I NEED TO SAY THIS...
WHEN WE FIRST MET, YOU MADE ME BELIEVE THAT THIS WORLD COULD CHANGE.
FOR THAT, I LOVED YOU.
YOU'RE ONE OF MY ONLY FRIENDS IN THIS WORLD.
I NEED YOU.
I CANNOT BE YOUR WORLD, NOT ANYMORE.
THE WORLD IS OUT THERE... AND IT NEEDS YOU.

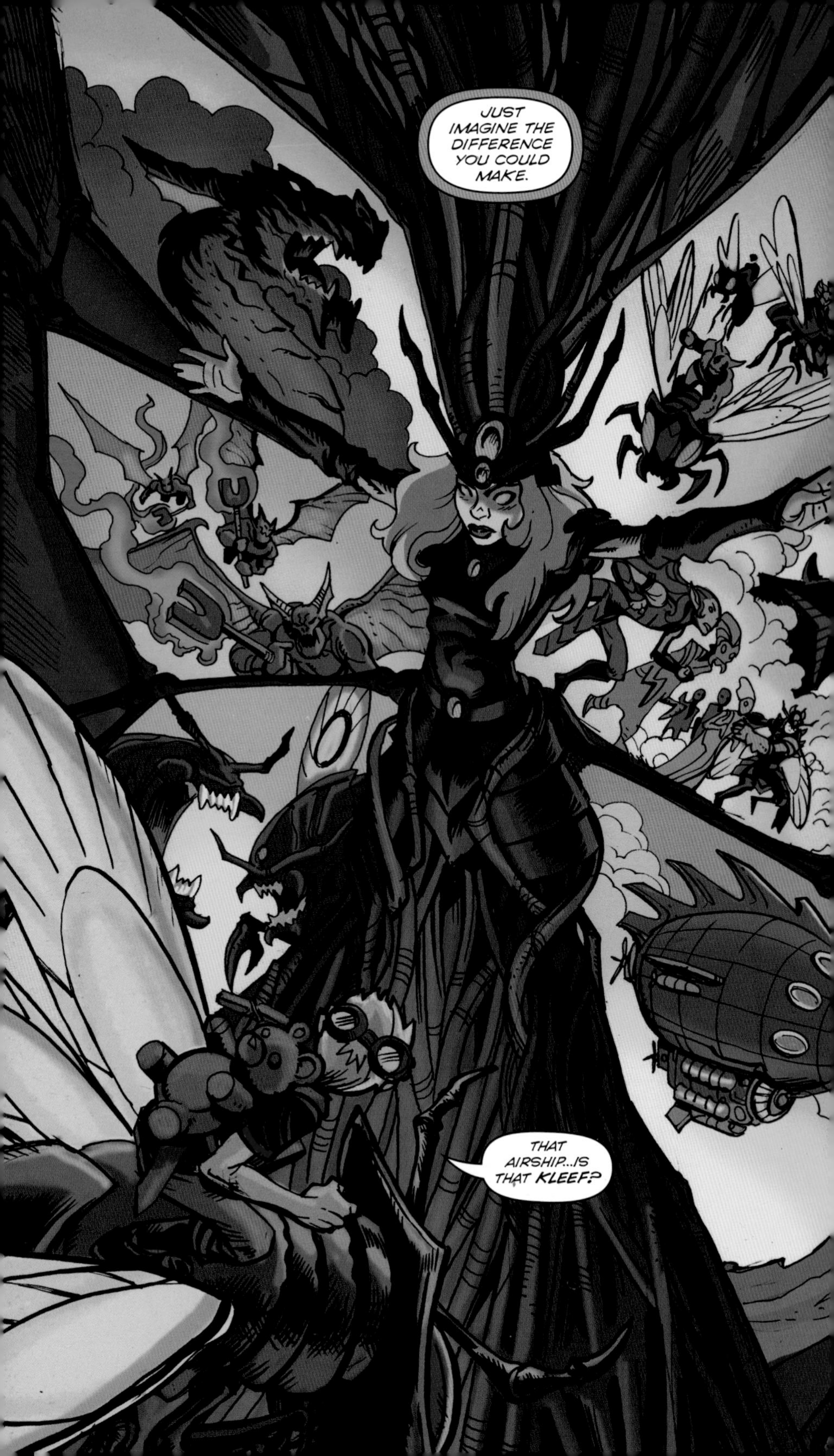
JUST IMAGINE THE DIFFERENCE YOU COULD MAKE.
THAT AIRSHIP...IS THAT KLEEF?

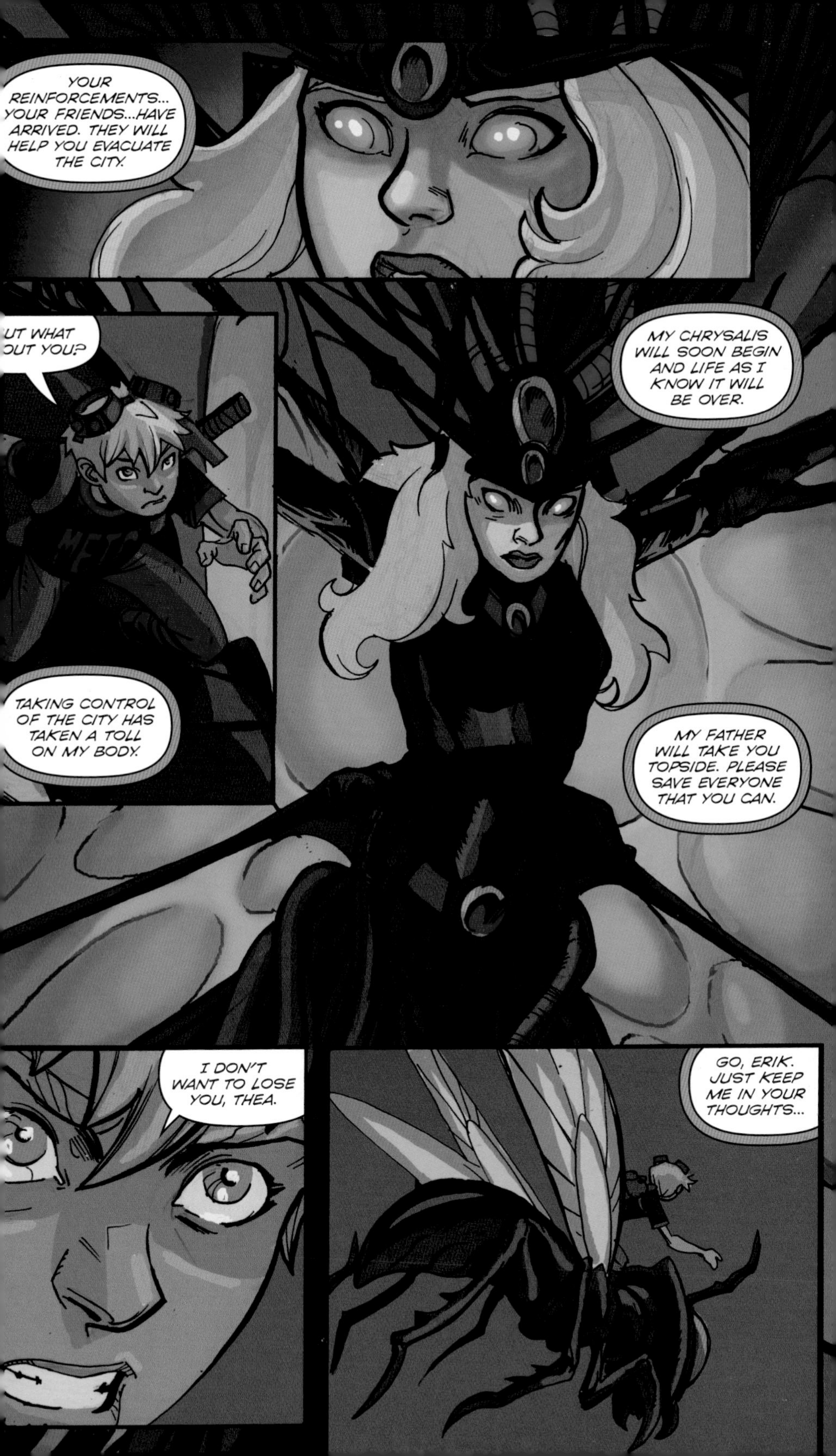
YOUR REINFORCEMENTS... YOUR FRIENDS...HAVE ARRIVED. THEY WILL HELP YOU EVACUATE THE CITY.
UT WHAT OUT YOU?
MY CHRYSALIS WILL SOON BEGIN AND LIFE AS I KNOW IT WILL BE OVER.
TAKING CONTROL OF THE CITY HAS TAKEN A TOLL ON MY BODY.
MY FATHER WILL TAKE YOU TOPSIDE. PLEASE SAVE EVERYONE THAT YOU CAN.
I DON'T WANT TO LOSE YOU, THEA.
GO, ERIK. JUST KEEP ME IN YOUR THOUGHTS...

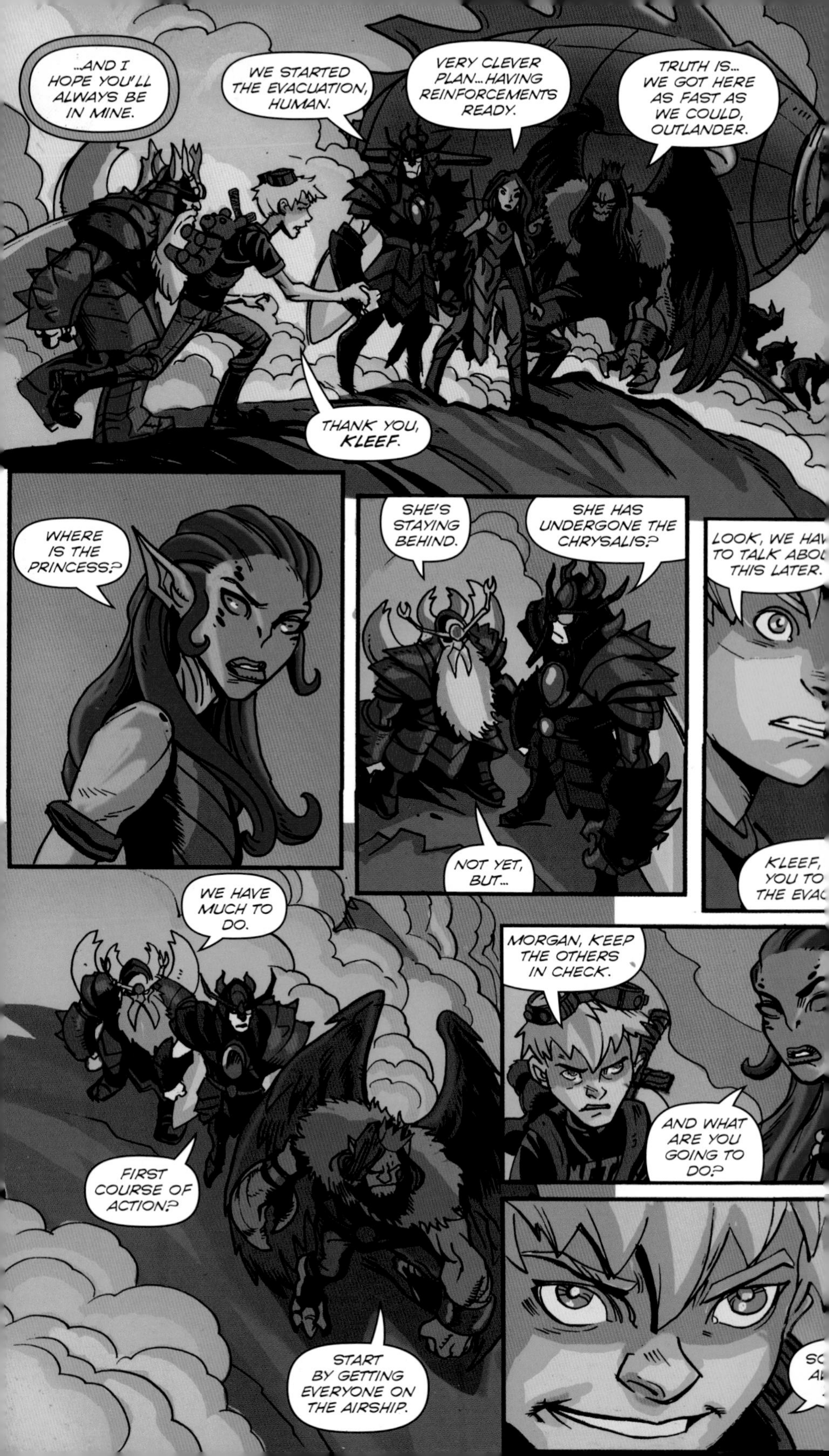
...AND I HOPE YOU'LL ALWAYS BE IN MINE.
WE STARTED THE EVACUATION, HUMAN.
VERY CLEVER PLAN... HAVING REINFORCEMENTS READY.
TRUTH IS... WE GOT HERE AS FAST AS WE COULD, OUTLANDER.
THANK YOU, KLEEF.
WHERE IS THE PRINCESS?
SHE'S STAYING BEHIND.
SHE HAS UNDERGONE THE CHRYSALIS?
NOT YET, BUT...
LOOK, WE HAV TO TALK ABO THIS LATER.
KLEEF, YOU TO THE EVA
WE HAVE MUCH TO DO.
FIRST COURSE OF ACTION?
START BY GETTING EVERYONE ON THE AIRSHIP.
MORGAN, KEEP THE OTHERS IN CHECK.
AND WHAT ARE YOU GOING TO DO?

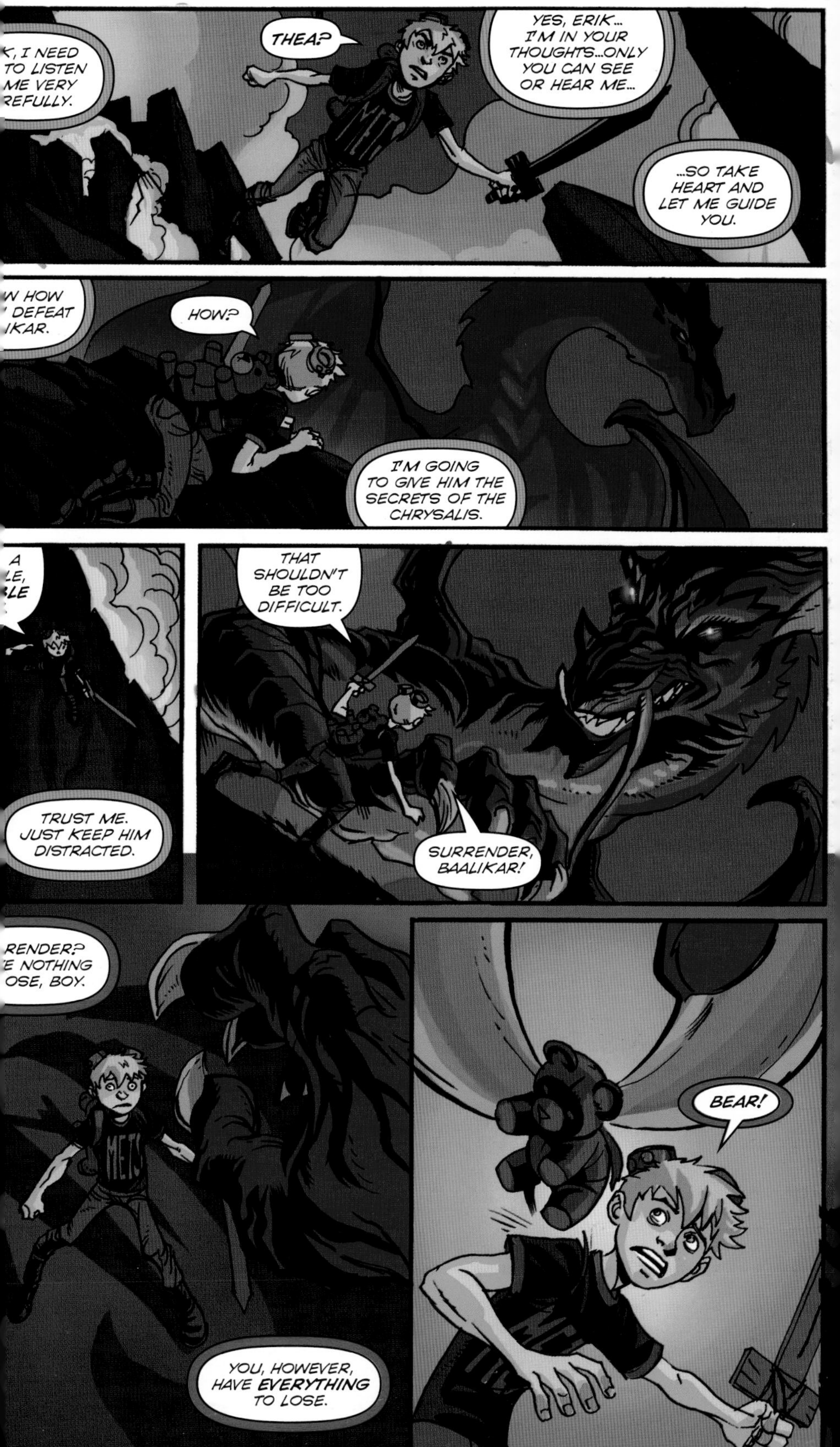
K, I NEED
TO LISTEN
ME VERY
REFULLY.
THEA?
YES, ERIK... I'M IN YOUR THOUGHTS...ONLY YOU CAN SEE OR HEAR ME...
...SO TAKE HEART AND LET ME GUIDE YOU.
W HOW
DEFEAT
IKAR.
HOW?
I'M GOING TO GIVE HIM THE SECRETS OF THE CHRYSALIS.
A
LE,
BLE
TRUST ME. JUST KEEP HIM DISTRACTED.
THAT SHOULDN'T BE TOO DIFFICULT.
SURRENDER, BAALIKAR!
RENDER?
E NOTHING
OSE, BOY.
YOU, HOWEVER, HAVE EVERYTHING TO LOSE.
BEAR!

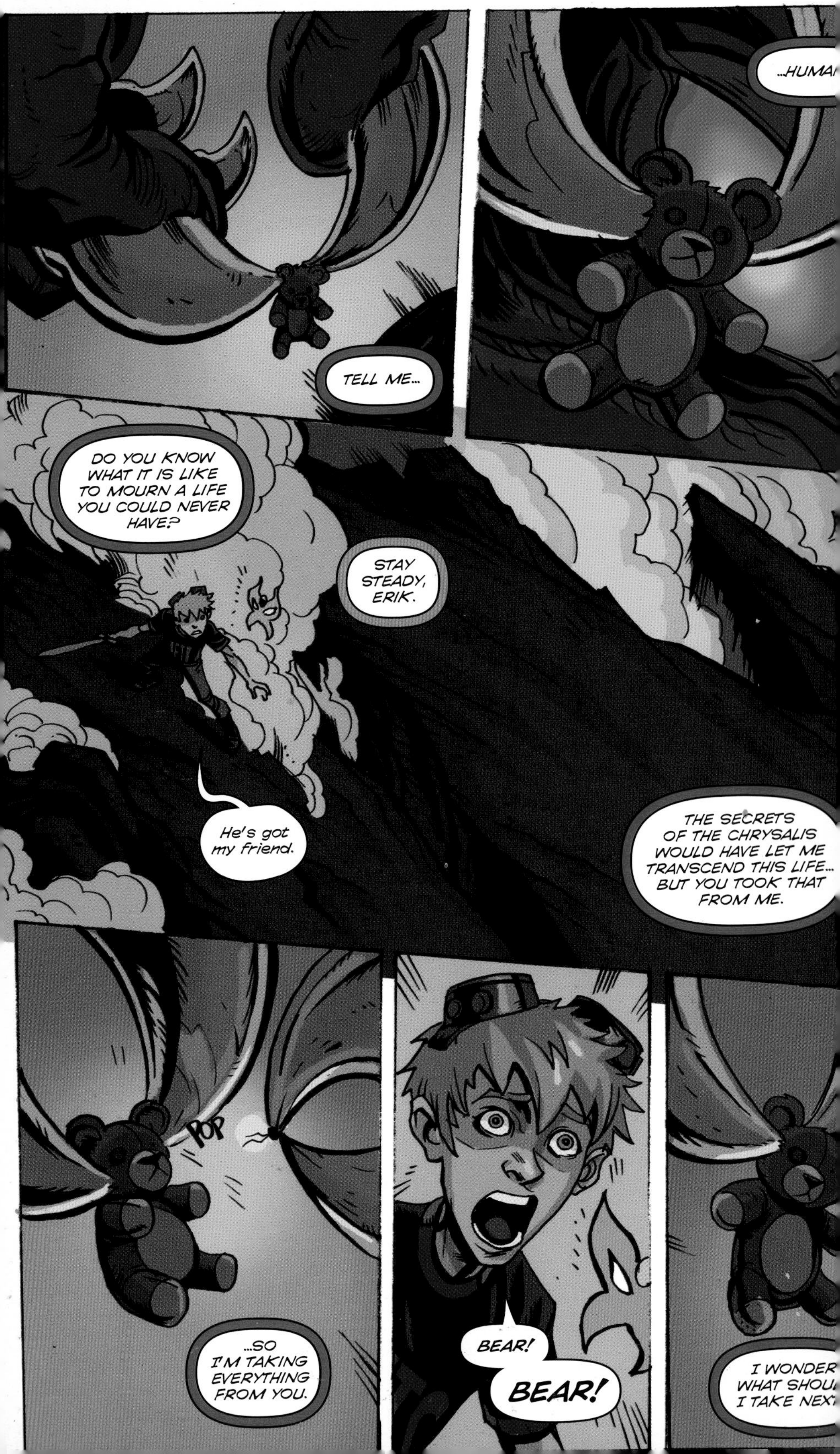
TELL ME...
...HUMA
DO YOU KNOW WHAT IT IS LIKE TO MOURN A LIFE YOU COULD NEVER HAVE?
STAY STEADY, ERIK.
He's got my friend.
THE SECRETS OF THE CHRYSALIS WOULD HAVE LET ME TRANSCEND THIS LIFE... BUT YOU TOOK THAT FROM ME.
POP
...SO I'M TAKING EVERYTHING FROM YOU.
BEAR!
BEAR!
I WONDER WHAT SHOU I TAKE NEX

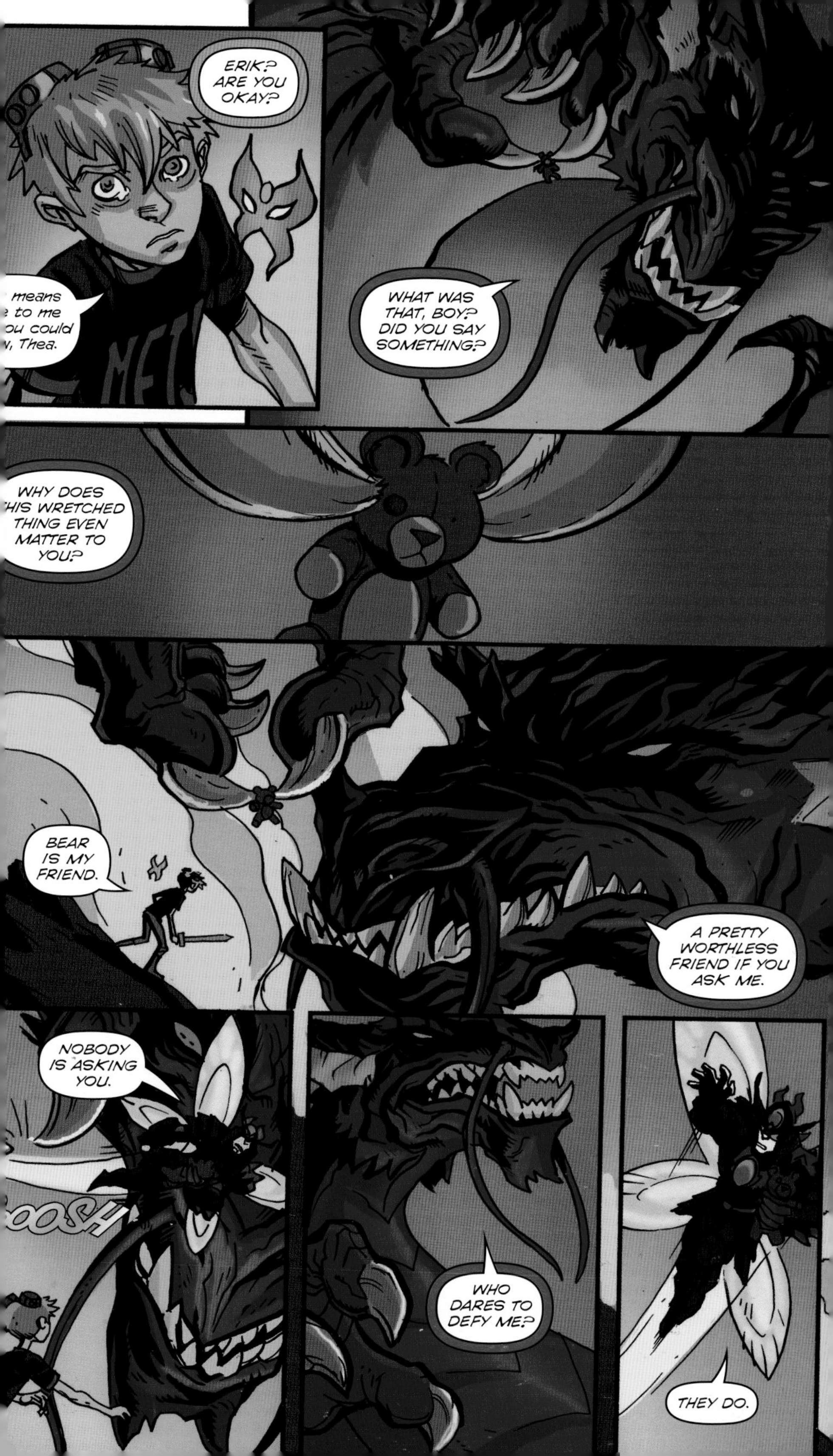
ERIK? ARE YOU OKAY?
means to me ou could , Thea.
WHAT WAS THAT, BOY? DID YOU SAY SOMETHING?
WHY DOES THIS WRETCHED THING EVEN MATTER TO YOU?
BEAR IS MY FRIEND.
A PRETTY WORTHLESS FRIEND IF YOU ASK ME.
NOBODY IS ASKING YOU.
OOSH
WHO DARES TO DEFY ME?
THEY DO.

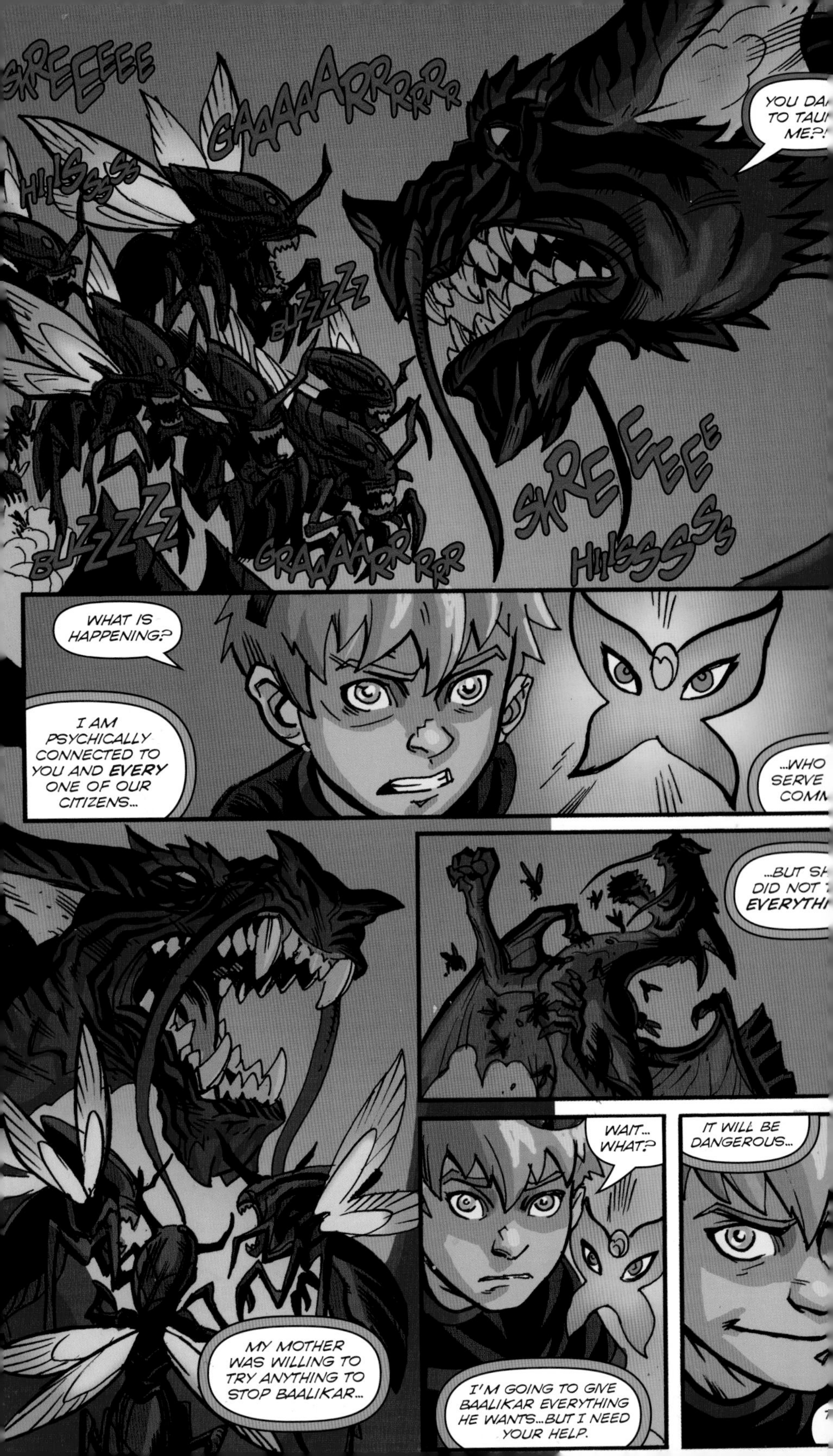
SKREEEEEE
GAAAAARRRRRRR
HIIISSSSS
YOU DA
TO TAU
ME?!
BUZZZZZ
SKREEEEEE
BUZZZZZ
GRAAAARRRRR
HIIISSSSS
WHAT IS HAPPENING?
I AM PSYCHICALLY CONNECTED TO YOU AND EVERY ONE OF OUR CITIZENS...
...WHO
SERVE
COMM
MY MOTHER WAS WILLING TO TRY ANYTHING TO STOP BAALIKAR...
...BUT SH
DID NOT
EVERYTH
WAIT... WHAT?
I'M GOING TO GIVE BAALIKAR EVERYTHING HE WANTS...BUT I NEED YOUR HELP.
IT WILL BE DANGEROUS...

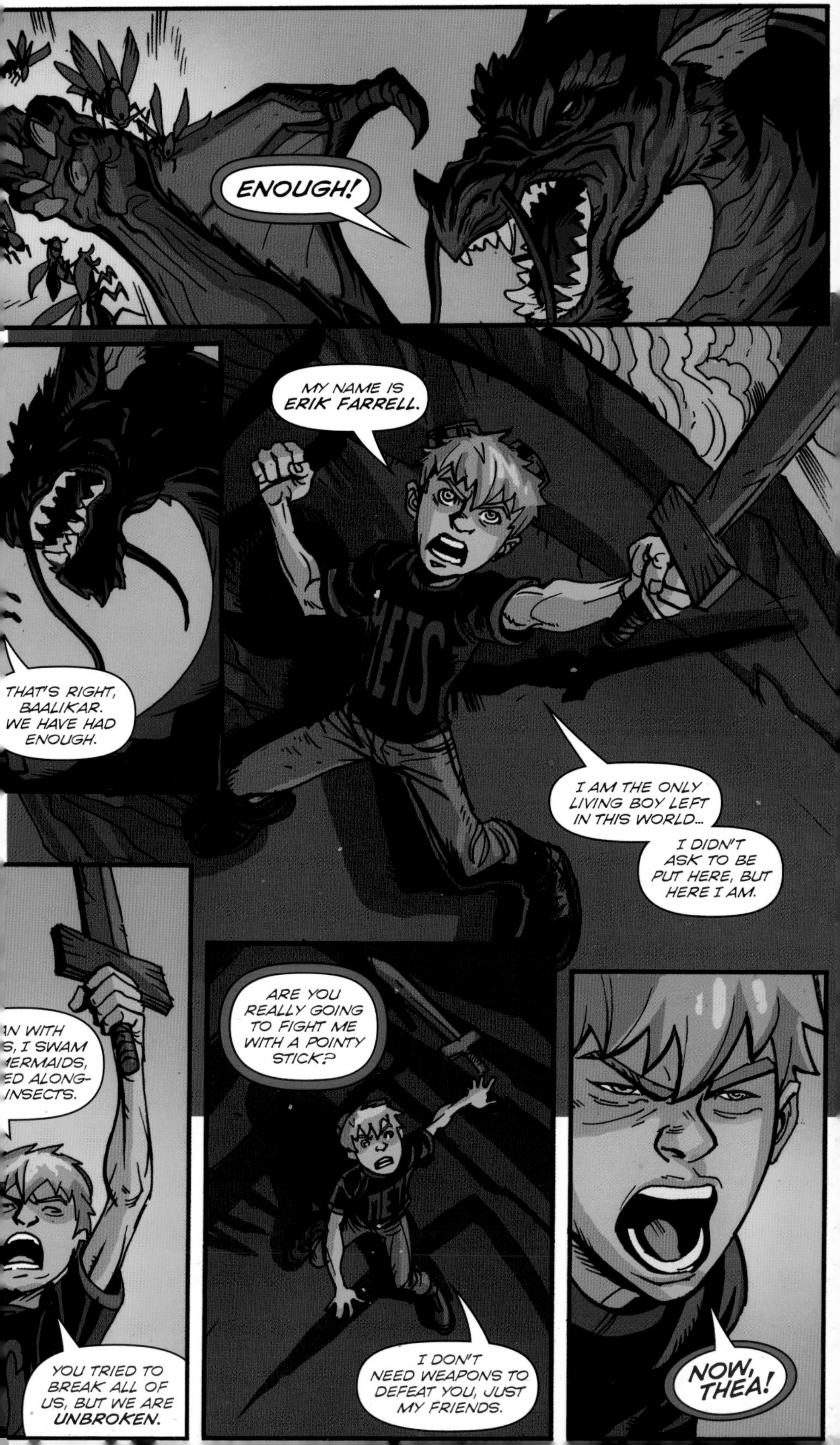
ENOUGH!
MY NAME IS ERIK FARRELL.
THAT'S RIGHT, BAALIKAR. WE HAVE HAD ENOUGH.
I AM THE ONLY LIVING BOY LEFT IN THIS WORLD...
I DIDN'T ASK TO BE PUT HERE, BUT HERE I AM.
AN WITH S, I SWAM MERMAIDS, ED ALONG- INSECTS.
YOU TRIED TO BREAK ALL OF US, BUT WE ARE UNBROKEN.
ARE YOU REALLY GOING TO FIGHT ME WITH A POINTY STICK?
I DON'T NEED WEAPONS TO DEFEAT YOU, JUST MY FRIENDS.
NOW, THEA!

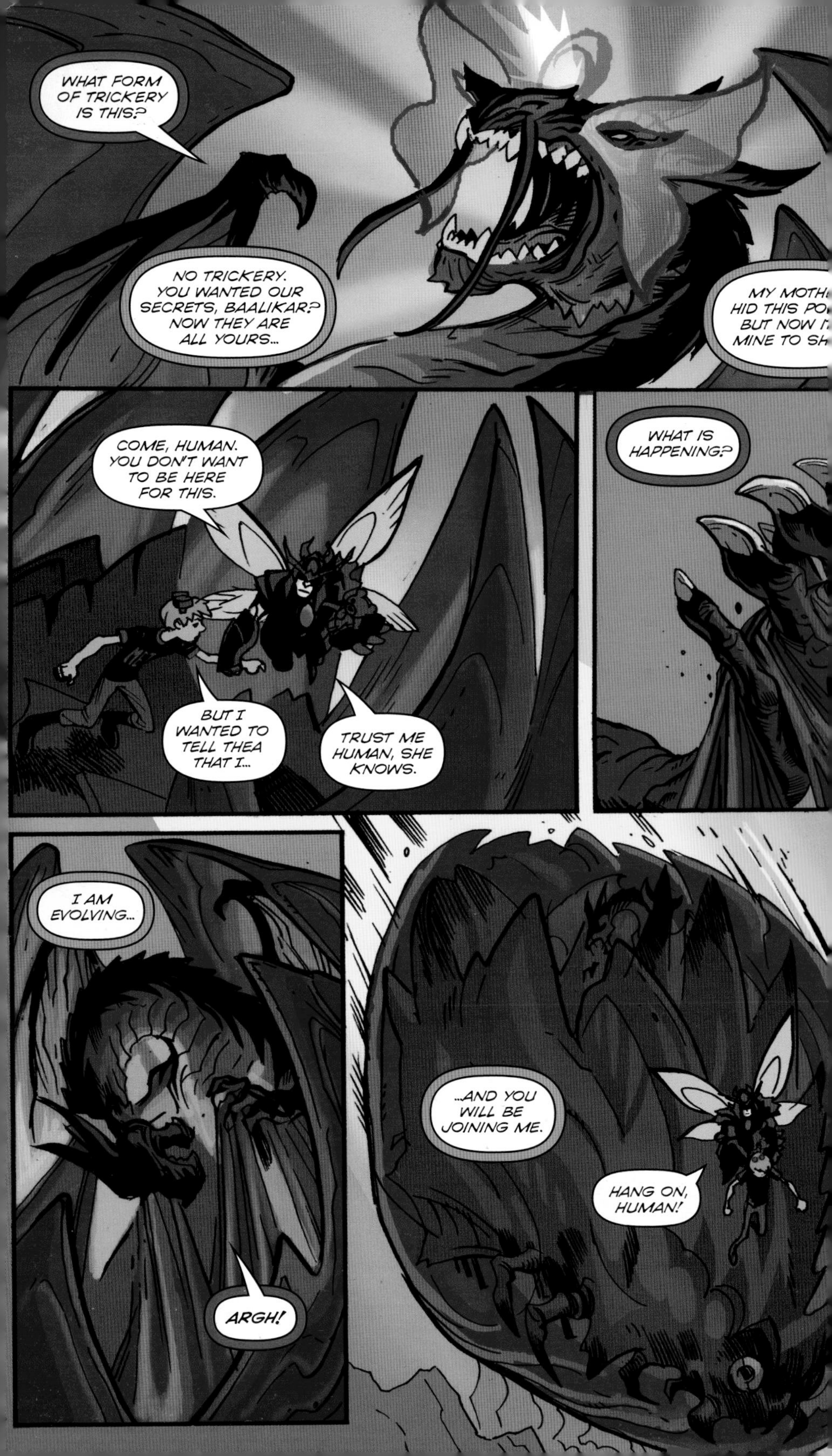
WHAT FORM OF TRICKERY IS THIS?
NO TRICKERY. YOU WANTED OUR SECRETS, BAALIKAR? NOW THEY ARE ALL YOURS...
COME, HUMAN. YOU DON'T WANT TO BE HERE FOR THIS.
BUT I WANTED TO TELL THEA THAT I...
TRUST ME HUMAN, SHE KNOWS.
WHAT IS HAPPENING?
I AM EVOLVING...
ARGH!
...AND YOU WILL BE JOINING ME.
HANG ON, HUMAN!

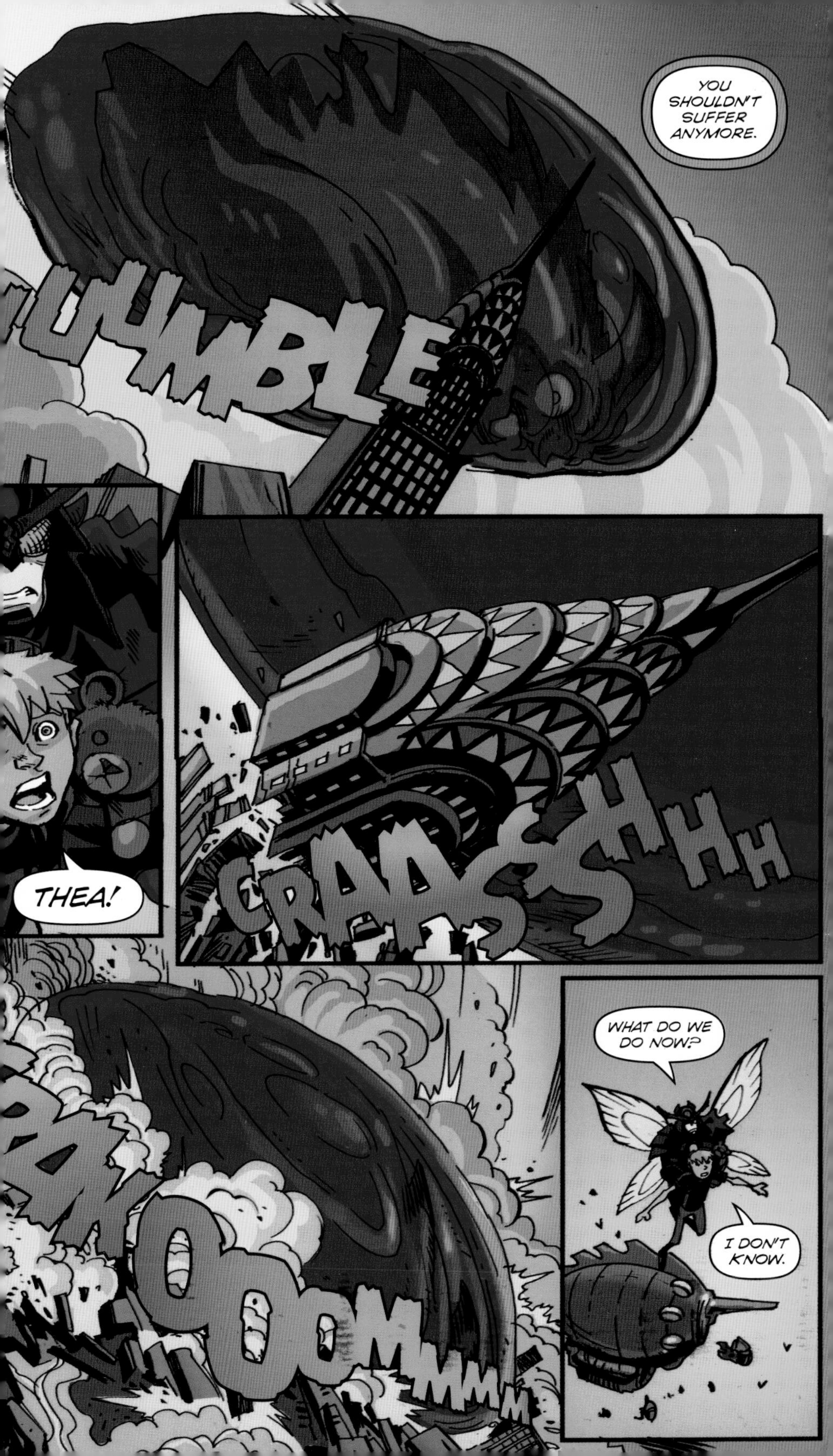
YOU SHOULDN'T SUFFER ANYMORE.
RUMBLE
THEA!
CRAASSHHH
WHAT DO WE DO NOW?
I DON'T KNOW.
OOOMMMM

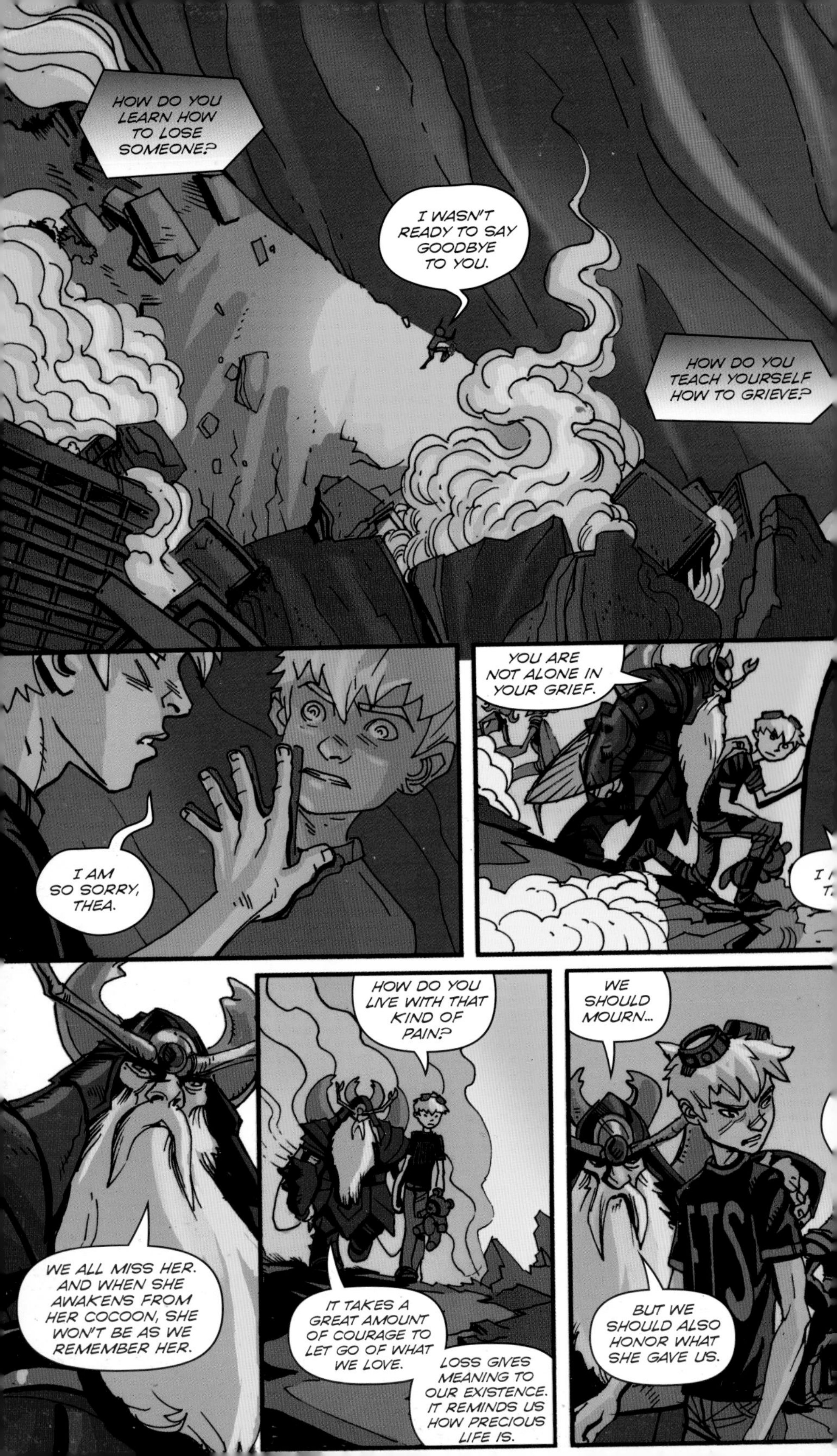
HOW DO YOU LEARN HOW TO LOSE SOMEONE?
I WASN'T READY TO SAY GOODBYE TO YOU.
HOW DO YOU TEACH YOURSELF HOW TO GRIEVE?
I AM SO SORRY, THEA.
YOU ARE NOT ALONE IN YOUR GRIEF.
WE ALL MISS HER. AND WHEN SHE AWAKENS FROM HER COCOON, SHE WON'T BE AS WE REMEMBER HER.
HOW DO YOU LIVE WITH THAT KIND OF PAIN?
IT TAKES A GREAT AMOUNT OF COURAGE TO LET GO OF WHAT WE LOVE.
LOSS GIVES MEANING TO OUR EXISTENCE. IT REMINDS US HOW PRECIOUS LIFE IS.
WE SHOULD MOURN...
BUT WE SHOULD ALSO HONOR WHAT SHE GAVE US.

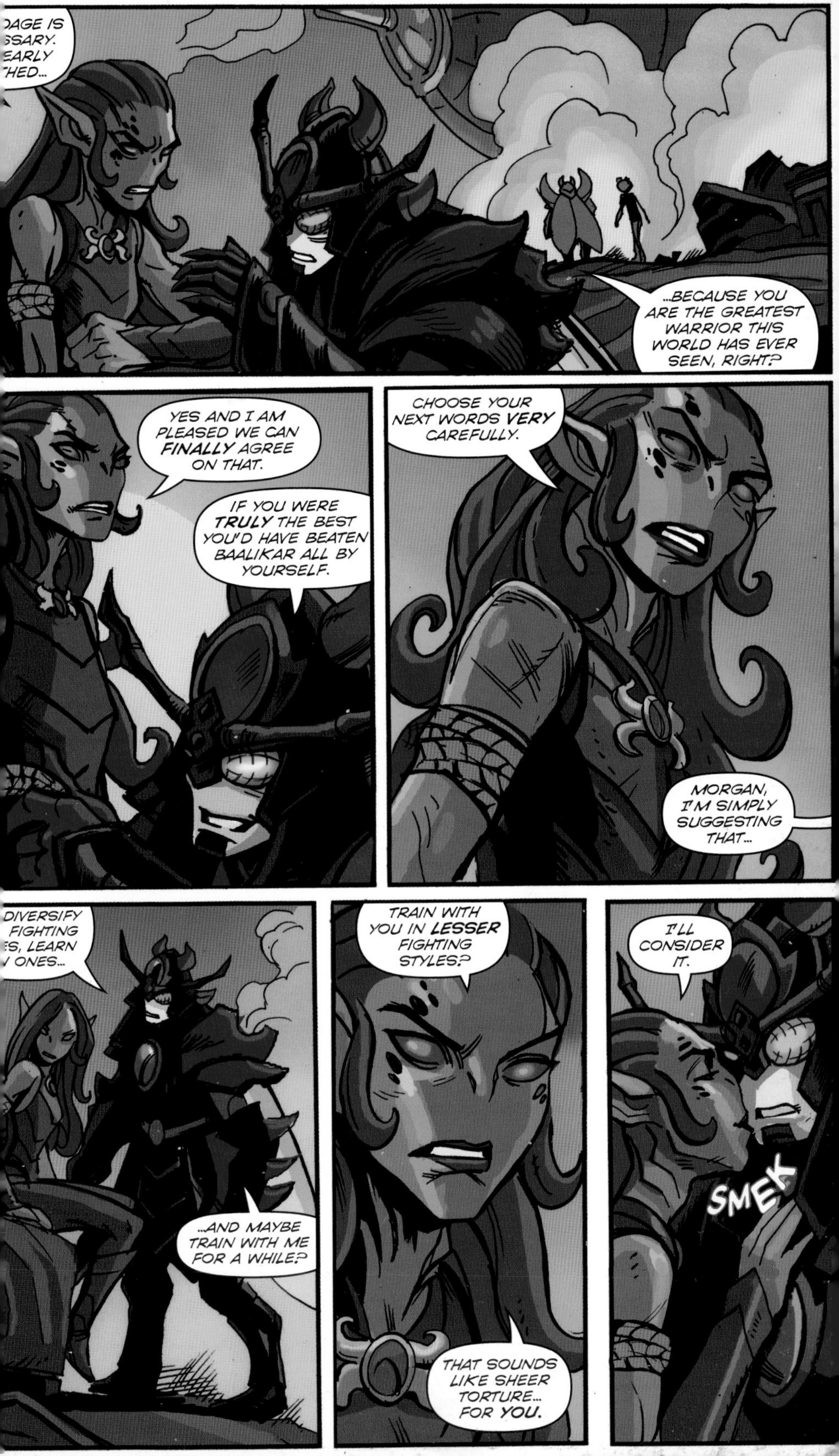

DAGE IS
SSARY.
EARLY
THED...
...BECAUSE YOU ARE THE GREATEST WARRIOR THIS WORLD HAS EVER SEEN, RIGHT?
YES AND I AM PLEASED WE CAN **FINALLY** AGREE ON THAT.
IF YOU WERE **TRULY** THE BEST YOU'D HAVE BEATEN BAALIKAR ALL BY YOURSELF.
CHOOSE YOUR NEXT WORDS **VERY** CAREFULLY.
MORGAN, I'M SIMPLY SUGGESTING THAT...
DIVERSIFY
FIGHTING
ES, LEARN
ONES...
...AND MAYBE TRAIN WITH ME FOR A WHILE?
TRAIN WITH YOU IN **LESSER** FIGHTING STYLES?
THAT SOUNDS LIKE SHEER TORTURE... FOR **YOU**.
I'LL CONSIDER IT.
SMEK

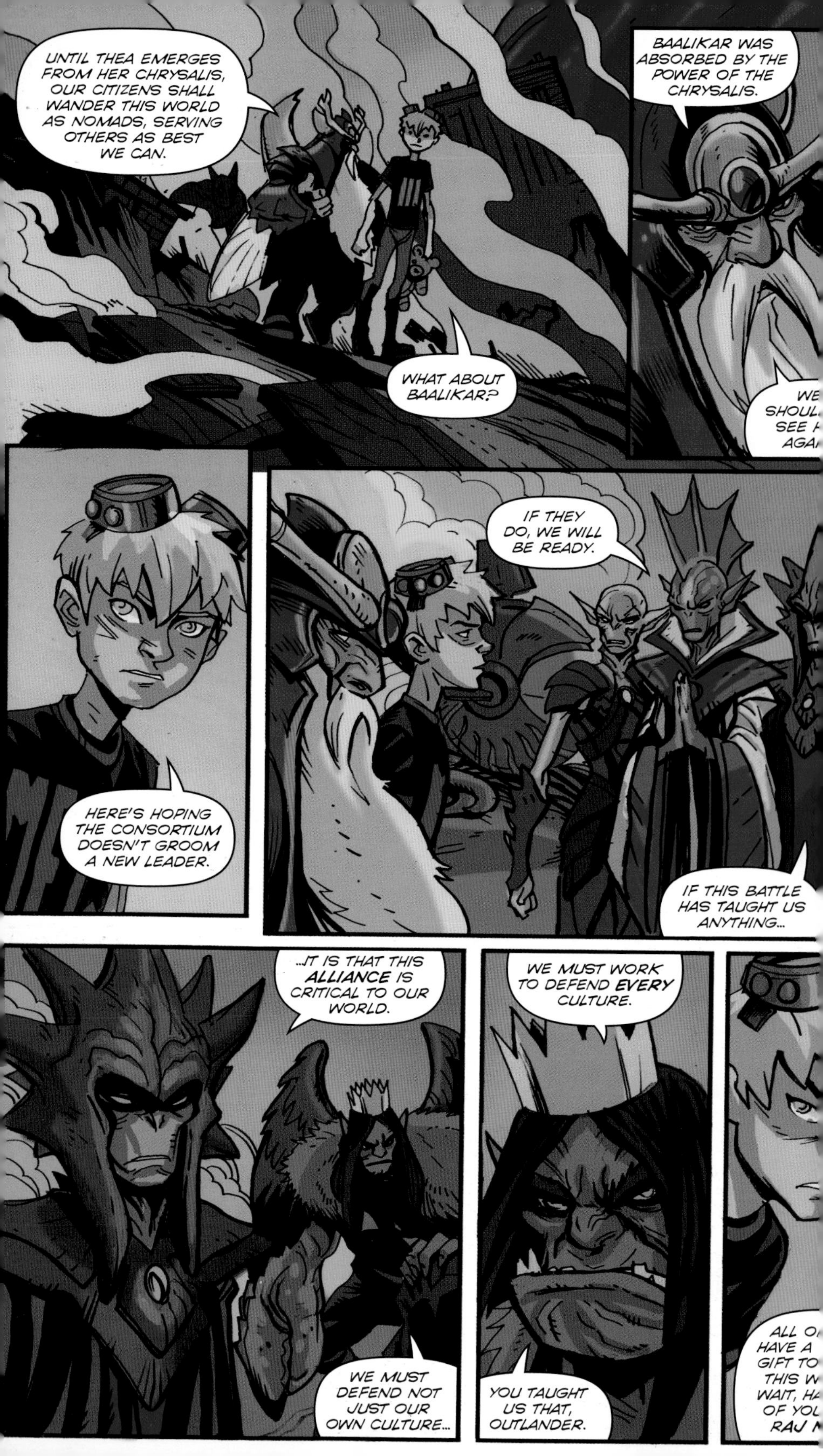
UNTIL THEA EMERGES FROM HER CHRYSALIS, OUR CITIZENS SHALL WANDER THIS WORLD AS NOMADS, SERVING OTHERS AS BEST WE CAN.
WHAT ABOUT BAALIKAR?
BAALIKAR WAS ABSORBED BY THE POWER OF THE CHRYSALIS.
HERE'S HOPING THE CONSORTIUM DOESN'T GROOM A NEW LEADER.
IF THEY DO, WE WILL BE READY.
IF THIS BATTLE HAS TAUGHT US ANYTHING...
...IT IS THAT THIS ALLIANCE IS CRITICAL TO OUR WORLD.
WE MUST DEFEND NOT JUST OUR OWN CULTURE...
WE MUST WORK TO DEFEND EVERY CULTURE.
YOU TAUGHT US THAT, OUTLANDER.

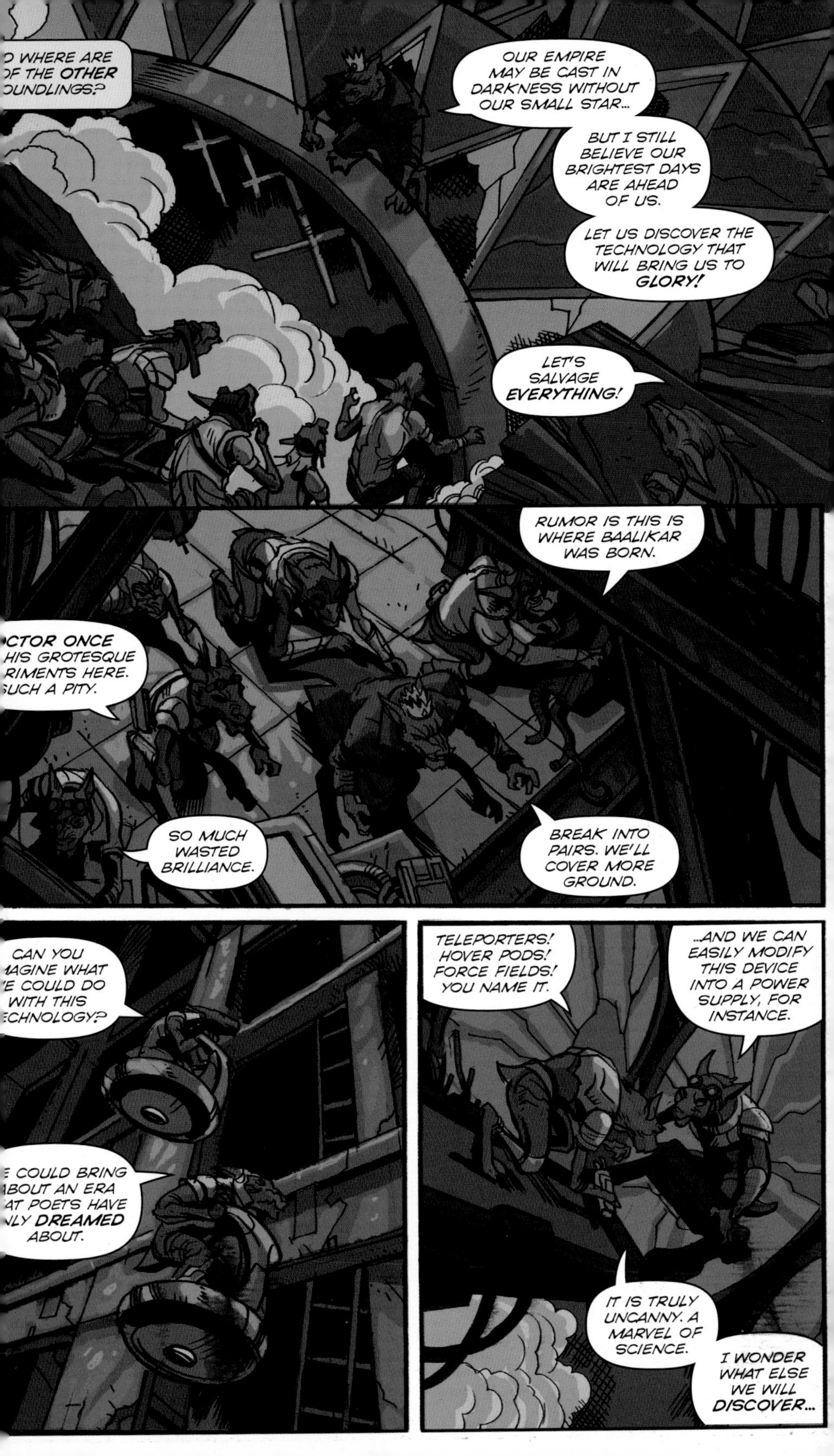

O WHERE ARE
OF THE OTHER
OUNDLINGS?
OUR EMPIRE MAY BE CAST IN DARKNESS WITHOUT OUR SMALL STAR...
BUT I STILL BELIEVE OUR BRIGHTEST DAYS ARE AHEAD OF US.
LET US DISCOVER THE TECHNOLOGY THAT WILL BRING US TO GLORY!
LET'S SALVAGE EVERYTHING!
RUMOR IS THIS IS WHERE BAALIKAR WAS BORN.
OCTOR ONCE
HIS GROTESQUE
RIMENTS HERE.
SUCH A PITY.
SO MUCH WASTED BRILLIANCE.
BREAK INTO PAIRS. WE'LL COVER MORE GROUND.
CAN YOU
MAGINE WHAT
E COULD DO
WITH THIS
ECHNOLOGY?
E COULD BRING
ABOUT AN ERA
AT POETS HAVE
NLY DREAMED
ABOUT.
TELEPORTERS! HOVER PODS! FORCE FIELDS! YOU NAME IT.
...AND WE CAN EASILY MODIFY THIS DEVICE INTO A POWER SUPPLY, FOR INSTANCE.
IT IS TRULY UNCANNY. A MARVEL OF SCIENCE.
I WONDER WHAT ELSE WE WILL DISCOVER...

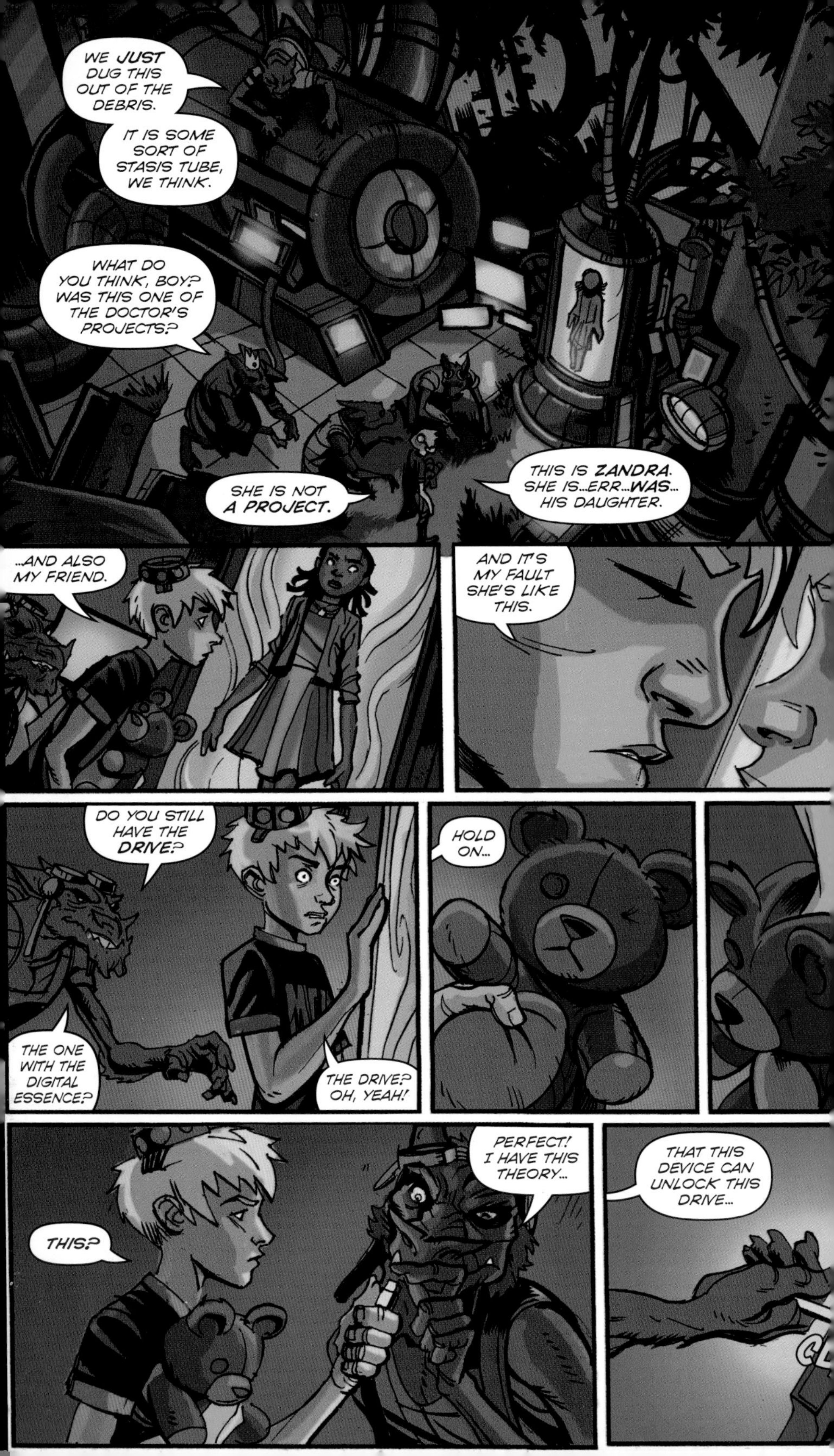
WE JUST DUG THIS OUT OF THE DEBRIS.
IT IS SOME SORT OF STASIS TUBE, WE THINK.
WHAT DO YOU THINK, BOY? WAS THIS ONE OF THE DOCTOR'S PROJECTS?
SHE IS NOT A PROJECT.
THIS IS ZANDRA. SHE IS...ERR...WAS... HIS DAUGHTER.
...AND ALSO MY FRIEND.
AND IT'S MY FAULT SHE'S LIKE THIS.
DO YOU STILL HAVE THE DRIVE?
THE ONE WITH THE DIGITAL ESSENCE?
THE DRIVE? OH, YEAH!
HOLD ON...
THIS?
PERFECT! I HAVE THIS THEORY...
THAT THIS DEVICE CAN UNLOCK THIS DRIVE...

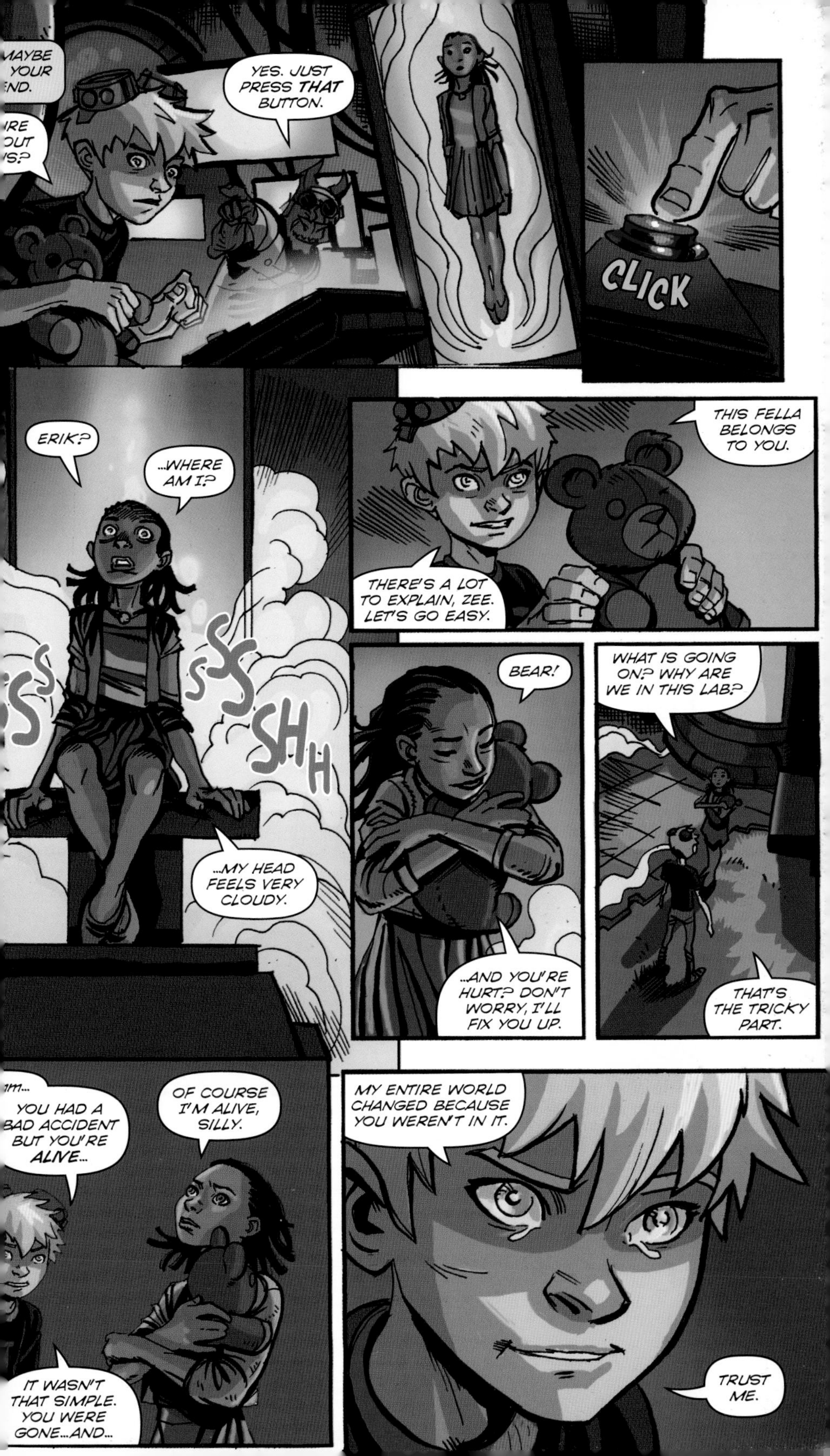
MAYBE YOUR ND.
RE OUT VS?
YES. JUST PRESS THAT BUTTON.
CLICK
ERIK?
...WHERE AM I?
SSSSSHH
...MY HEAD FEELS VERY CLOUDY.
THIS FELLA BELONGS TO YOU.
THERE'S A LOT TO EXPLAIN, ZEE. LET'S GO EASY.
BEAR!
...AND YOU'RE HURT? DON'T WORRY, I'LL FIX YOU UP.
WHAT IS GOING ON? WHY ARE WE IN THIS LAB?
THAT'S THE TRICKY PART.
m... YOU HAD A BAD ACCIDENT BUT YOU'RE ALIVE...
OF COURSE I'M ALIVE, SILLY.
IT WASN'T THAT SIMPLE. YOU WERE GONE...AND...
MY ENTIRE WORLD CHANGED BECAUSE YOU WEREN'T IN IT.
TRUST ME.

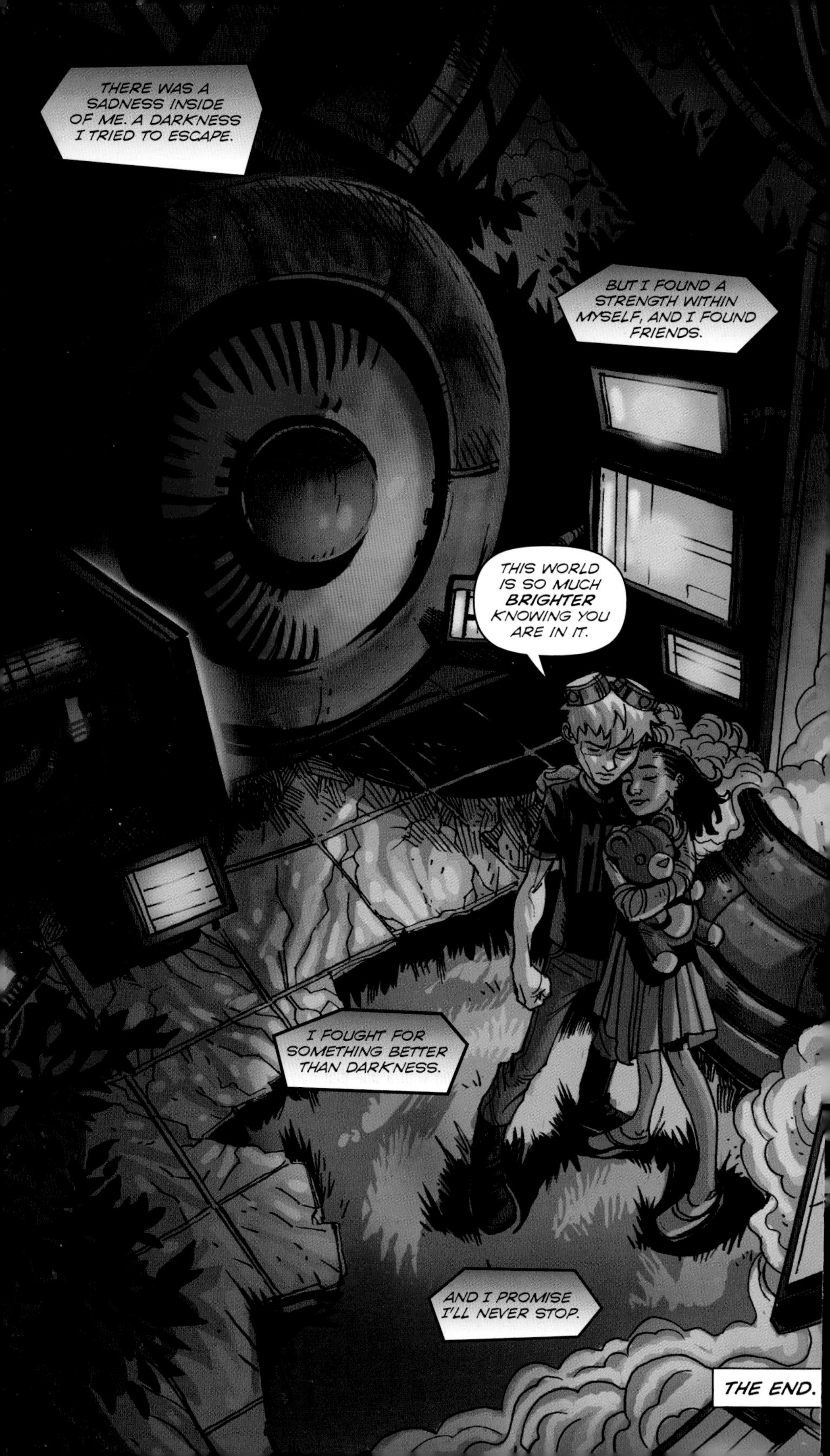
THERE WAS A SADNESS INSIDE OF ME. A DARKNESS I TRIED TO ESCAPE.
BUT I FOUND A STRENGTH WITHIN MYSELF, AND I FOUND FRIENDS.
THIS WORLD IS SO MUCH BRIGHTER KNOWING YOU ARE IN IT.
I FOUGHT FOR SOMETHING BETTER THAN DARKNESS.
AND I PROMISE I'LL NEVER STOP.
THE END.

WATCH OUT FOR PAPERCUTZ™

...ne to the fifth and final (for now!) THE ONLY LIVING BOY graphic novel, by David Gallaher and Steve Ellis, from ...utz–those fearless entrepreneurs dedicated to publishing great graphic novels for all ages. I'm Jim Salicrup, ...in-Chief and Resident Eternal Optimist, here to offer some miscellaneous musings...

...all just witnessed Erik Farrell's heroic journey to the Patchwork Planet and his epic battles against Doctor Once and ...r–pretty powerful stuff. But each and every one of us is on a journey, and we're all facing various obstacles on a daily ...That's even true for a small independent publishing company such as Papercutz. While we've had many successes ...e years, the reality is that it's very challenging to keep going. While nowhere near as deadly as what Erik faces, the ...les we face can be pretty scary at times–after all, there's no guarantee that we'll always be in business. We have to ...ard every day making sure we deliver graphic novels that you really want to see. THE ONLY LIVING BOY is a perfect ...le of the kind of material we love–a powerful story, brilliantly written and beautifully drawn. Writer David Gallaher and ...teve Ellis take their work very seriously, creating a story that respects the intelligence of its audience. Working with ...nd Steve has been both a real honor and pleasure for us at Papercutz.

...at's why we're happy to announce a new graphic novel series from our Papercutz imprint for older audiences, Super ...: HIGH MOON by David Gallaher and Steve Ellis. The creators of THE ONLY LIVING BOY have created a supernatural ...set in the Old West, and Super Genius will be publishing it. We're mentioning it here because the audience for THE ONLY ...BOY includes a fair amount of fans old enough to pick up a Super Genius title, and we wanted you to be aware that it ...But fair warning, HIGH MOON is NOT an all-ages title, and is suggested for mature audiences only.

...se wondering exactly what Super Genius is, allow me to explain... Not long ago, Papercutz introduced an imprint ...ed to publish material for older audiences called Super Genius. Recent titles have included the Eisner Award-nominated ...e-fiction series TRISH TRASH, by writer/artist Jessica Abel; an interesting reinvention of the Peter Pan story called THE ...Y PROJECT, by writer Melissa Jane Osborne and artist Veronica Fish; a beautifully painted adaptation of the Jules Verne ...THE CHILDREN OF CAPTAIN GRANT, by writer/artist Alexis Nesme; an all-new version of the legendary horror comic, ...FROM THE CRYPT; and collected editions of LADY JUSTICE, TEKNOPHAGE, and MR HERO, all characters created ...t-selling author Neil Gaiman. Super Genius even has a graphic novel coming up that will tell the true-life story of Joe ...r, the co-creator of Superman–talk about a true Super Genius!

...ately, Papercutz continues to publish graphic novels that are able to beat the odds and find appreciative audiences. A ...cent examples are THE LOUD HOUSE, a graphic novel series based on the award-winning, hit Nickelodeon animated ...created by Chris Savino. It's about young Lincoln Loud, the only boy in a family that has eleven children. Lincoln's ...ures are far more down-to-earth than Erik Farrell's, and a whole lot funnier. Unrelated, THE SISTERS focuses on just ...lings, Wendy and her younger sister Maureen, but they somehow manage to create just as much chaos as the Louds! ...nk you'll enjoy this series by Cazenove and William–which includes occasional flights of fancy with Wendy and Maureen ...e themselves as The Super Sisters!

...to also mention HOTEL TRANSYLVANIA, THE ZODIAC LEGACY, DRACULA MARRIES FRANKENSTEIN, MANOSAURS, ...S, and many other Papercutz titles, but I thought I'd end with a title that may be just the thing to enjoy after five ...s of THE ONLY LIVING BOY...GUMBY! While Erik Farrell had to dig down deep into his soul to face nightmarish ...rs, GUMBY is all about the joy of being alive and appreciating the simpler pleasures of life. We've assembled an all-star ...of comics creators–Kyle Baker, Art Baltazar, Ray Fawkes, Veronica Fish, Sholly Fisch, Rick Geary, Mike Kazaleh, Jeff ...an, Jolyon Yates, and others–to create the all-new adventures of everyone's favorite clayboy, and we hope you check it ...ter suffering through all the havoc caused by Doctor Once and Baalikar, dealing with mischief created by those goofy ...eads will be downright fun.

...ed at above, Erik Farrell will return. And his adventure ...ntinue. Be sure to keep your eye on papercutz.com for ...ws regarding THE ONLY LIVING BOY. So until we meet ...be sure to watch out for Papercutz!

Thanks, *Jim*

STAY IN TOUCH!

EMAIL:	salicrup@papercutz.com
WEB:	papercutz.com
INSTAGRAM:	@papercutzgn
TWITTER:	@papercutzgn
FACEBOOK:	PAPERCUTZGRAPHICNOVELS
FAN MAIL:	Papercutz, 160 Broadway, Suite 700, East Wing, New York, NY 10038

AFTERWORD

THE ONLY LIVING BOY began as an impossible idea. How does a boy and his teddy bear backpack navigate a world filled with monsters, mayhem and mad science? That impossible idea became thousands of words and illustrations — and the basis for the book you hold in your hand.

Bringing this part of the adventure to a close is something that we thought would happen in the distant future. But here we are, on the very last page — and it has never been more difficult to say goodbye.

When we look back at THE ONLY LIVING BOY — and the journey that Erik, Morgan, and Thea took together, our hearts are filled with joy. This has been an incredible adventure for us and it wouldn't be possible if it wasn't for the outstanding work of our agent, Dara Hyde, the diligence of our publicist, David Hyde, the exceptional work of our studio, the hardworking talent from the team at Papercutz, and the love from both our families and our exceptional fans — like you.

The world is an uncertain place. We are, all of us, trying to make sense of a world that makes no sense at all. That uncertainty can swallow us whole — and make us feel inadequate. The world doesn't make it easy for us to be brave. We often find ourselves too afraid to fail and too afraid to make a difference.

Erik Farrell is a scared kid who found himself too often running away from his problems. The world that he stumbled into was even more uncertain and senseless. With Bear by his side, he had to talk himself into being brave, even if it meant that he'd make mistakes. And... well, he makes a lot of mistakes. But if there is one lesson that we want you to take from this series, it is this: failure is better than never trying at all.

The world — our world — is weird, wide, and wonderful... and it's yours to explore alone or with your friends. It's okay to be scared. It's okay to be sad. It's okay to be filled with anger. Don't be afraid of your emotions, of your ambition, or even of your dreams — those are primal forces. Harness them to make the impossible possible. All you need is the certainty inside of you.

We will be back with new stories to tell. Thank you for believing in us as we told this one...